The Complete

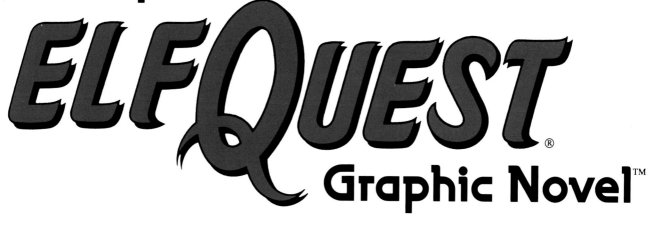

Graphic Novel™

Book Six:
The Secret of Two-Edge

by Wendy and Richard Pini

coloring by Chelsea Animation Studio, New York
supervised by Wendy Pini

FATHER TREE PRESS • Poughkeepsie, New York • 1989

The Complete Elfquest Graphic Novel

Book Six: The Secret of Two-Edge

Published by Father Tree Press, a division of Warp Graphics, Inc.

For **the friends, the co-workers, the fans, the families and tribes** without whom the shade would have been less cool, the water less sweet

Color separations by Colorifics, Inc., San Antonio, Texas
Printed in the United States of America by Hart Graphics, Austin, Texas

First printing February 1989
10 9 8 7 6 5 4 3 2 1
ISBN 0-936861-11-8 (pbk.)

Introduction

by Walter & Louise Simonson

We've never written an introduction for anything before, so when Richard asked us to write one for this volume of the *Elfquest* Graphic Novels, we decided we'd better do a little homework. We thought long and hard about elves, *Elfquest*, independent comics companies (whatever *that* means!), licensed properties, work-for-hire, and all sorts of good clean party things. We managed to cadge the anniversary volumes out of the Pinis (not as a bribe, you understand, but purely for research purposes...), read all the introductions, and made a terrifying discovery. Pretty much everything we were going to say, or thought of saying, or even considered saying had already been said! The previous intro writers had already spoken of how the books are filled with passion (and compassion), of how the characters ring true whether the reader is human or elf, and so on and so on in a depressing litany of exact correspondence. In other words, all the big, important stuff had been said already.

Which left us with one of two choices: Either we write the shortest introduction on record (and we've already blown that!), or we find something else to say.

So what follows here is a little small-scale personal history, not trumpeting the measure of Wendy and Richard's achievement, nor examining their place in the eventual history of the medium, or anything else that rings of formal cultural significance, but something that we think is appropriate for a comic book and especially, for *this* comic. Because after all is said and done, we read comics by ourselves. One to one. Oh, we may sing their praises to friends, share them with our buddies, send our contributions to fanzines, form our clubs, and take part in a hundred other communal activities that surround comics but in the end...in the end, we read comics alone. We experience their wonder and their magic on an intimate level. The pictures and the words speak directly to us. The creator and the reader become water brothers of the page.

It is one of the universal traits of comics fans that they are compelled to be ruthlessly honest whenever they are confronted by a professional in the field. Tact, grace, diplomacy, common courtesy, all of these must take a back seat before the fan's overwhelming urge to explain, elucidate, critique and criticize the work of the artist or writer before him. This is true of comics fans everywhere without exception, as any professional will tell you. When Richard spoke to us about writing this introduction, he had only one request: that we not write a puff piece. And with that, of course, he gave us sanction to lay aside our professional hats and speak openly with the blunt honesty every fan takes for granted.

The truth is that I don't read comics much any more. And by "any more" I mean I have read very few comics over the past seventeen years, which is about how long I've been working professionally in the field. That doesn't mean I don't have *some* idea of what's going on. I've become pseudo-literate in comics the way I was once pseudo-knowledgeable about *Saturday Night Live*. That show, for me, was a fairly uninteresting hour and a half of viewing punctuated by white hot flashes of hilarity. But I didn't feel like watching that much TV for so little reward. And I found I didn't have to. Inevitably, a day or two after each show, any one of a number of friends, acquaintances, casual passersby or total strangers would buttonhole me for five or ten minutes and regale me with instant replays of the hot flashes. Which meant I could keep up with one of the cultural icons of an era and not have to spend much time doing it. It was great!

That's about how I handle comics. In fairness, however, we should note here that the Weezie half of the couple writing this introduction actually *does* keep up with a number of comics titles. She also finishes her homework when she's supposed to, and generally has a good handle on what's happening.

All of which is by way of saying that when *Elfquest* began coming out, the Walter half of the couple didn't leap to the fore, rush out and buy 50 copies of the first issue, or shout its virtue from the rooftops. This even though friends kept telling me how good it was and what a jerk I was for not checking it out. Copies did find their way into our apartment but went unread by me. Not so for my loving and devoted wife. She tried one issue, then consumed the rest as they came into the house. (She thought I was a jerk, too.)

Time passed. And I slowly became aware of the fact that we had not one but *two* readers of *Elfquest* in the house! Weezie persuaded our kid, Julianna, to take a look at the comic. And suddenly Juli (who wasn't reading much of anything in those days) was not only reading the comic but devouring it. She, in turn, sucked her best friends into the world of Cutter, Leetah, et al. The circle widened to include other friends as well. Weezie sent a set of *Elfquest*s to our ever-increasing hoard of nieces one Christmas. Which is essentially how *Elfquest* works.

Insidiously.

Of course, I was also the victim of my own prejudices. *Elfquest*? Obviously girl stuff (no offense, Richard). Give me some of those bone crunching, teeth jarring, manly SUPERHERO comics any time! (Not that I was reading many of them, but you catch my drift.)

But I finally broke down and read a couple of issues in a weak moment. And a couple more. And finished reading everything else we had in one sitting. And then I was crabby because the Pinis hadn't completed the first series at the time and that mean I had to wait for the last few issues like everybody else!

The point isn't that *Elfquest* drew our family closer together in some gentle, charming and sappy fashion (although we *were* all crabby in unison waiting for the final issues). But each of us experienced the book on that intimate scale I spoke of earlier. And responded to it. *Elfquest* managed to be both a private pleasure and a public avalanche. (And if you doubt me, just hop on your time-cycle and drop by the 1981 San Diego Comic convention when there seemed to be *thousands* of elaborately costumed elves dashing hither and thither throughout the convention center!)

Such a personal *and* communal response is rare in comics. It's rare in any fiction. It means that the creators' voices have spoken the words that transmute fiction into life. And those voices resonate back to the dawn of man, when the first storyteller sat before the fire that kept the wild things at bay and spoke of hidden treasures and of the human heart.

We haven't talked with Wendy and Richard lately so we don't know if they're ready to run screaming into the hills around Poughkeepsie at the merest hint of anything remotely elf-related in their futures. It's possible; fictitious worlds can be hard and demanding masters. But we hope not. And we suspect not. Once the elf is out of the bottle, it's mighty tough to get it back in again!

Which is fine by us. We'd like to see the saga of *Elfquest* continue. We're greedy that way.

SIEGE AT BLUE MOUNTAIN

ARTIST/WRITER	CO-PLOT/EDITOR	PART	INKS	GUEST LETTERER
WENDY PINI	RICHARD PINI	5	JOE STATON	CLEM ROBINS

STRAINING AGAINST THE WIND AS HER WINGED MOUNT SUDDENLY DIVES TOWARD THE GROUND, *AROREE* DOES NOT ATTEMPT TO REGAIN HER NORTHWARD COURSE.

SHE KNOWS THE MOODS OF THE GIGANTIC BIRD OF PREY SHE RIDES.

THERE ARE LIMITS TO THE CONTROL HER BOND WITH HIM GIVES HER--PARTICULARLY WHEN HE IS VERY HUNGRY.

SHE HAS FLOWN HIM FAR AND FAST ON HER PILGRIMAGE TO THE PALACE OF THE HIGH ONES.

NOW IT IS TIME FOR HIM TO *FEED*.

LITTLETRILL...! WHAT HAVE YOU SPOTTED DOWN THERE?

AAWWK!

2

AAAHHH! YAHAAA!

SOB

AAWWW! BETTER SAVE HIGH-DIG-DIG!

HOLD, PRESERVER! ...DOESN'T THAT GREAT HAWK BELONG TO...

--A GLIDER!?

OH, THE *HIGH ONES* ARE WITH ME TODAY!

DISCREETLY, **RAYEK** HOVERS AS TALL **ARÓREE** DISMOUNTS WITH A NATIVE LIGHTNESS THAT HE, DESPITE YEARS OF PRACTICE, HAS YET TO APPROACH. HIS ADMIRATION OF HER IS TINGED WITH ENVY.

PETALWING!

HELLO, PRETTY FLYHIGHTHING!

RAWK!! RAWK!

THE CLAWS! HE CRUSHES ME!!

HEEELLP!

3

4

SILENTLY *RAYEK* STUDIES THE FEAR-HAUNTED GLIDER AS SHE COAXES THE GREAT BIRD'S CLAWS OPEN.

THEN...

BUT I AM *NOT* A STRANGER TO YOUR PEOPLE'S TROUBLES, MAIDEN.

I KNOW OF YOUR *LORD VOLL'S* DEATH--

--ƎUHNƎ AND OF *WINNOWILL!*

THEN YOU KNOW WELL ENOUGH TO STAY FAR AWAY FROM HER!

AARK!

EVER SINCE *VOLL* DIED, *SHE* HAS BEEN OUR LORD. AND WE, EVEN TO THE LEAST GIFTED OF US, HAVE BEEN BOUND BY HER FOR A PURPOSE SOMEHOW CONNECTED TO THE GREAT *EGG.* OUR MAGIC IS HERS TO COMMAND--

"--AS *YOURS* WILL BE, DARK SKINNED ONE, IF YOU FALL INTO *WINNOWILL'S* HANDS!"

TSK! POOR CREATURE! SHE HAS THE RIGHT IDEA, FOCUSING THE COMBINED POWERS OF THE GLIDERS ON SOME TASK OR OTHER...BUT SHE GOES ABOUT IT IN THE WRONG WAY!

HER GOALS AND MINE, I SUSPECT, ARE SIMILAR. I'D SAY SHE HAS NEED OF ME.

5

I HAVE A FEELING THE MOONS WILL RISE AND SET MANY TIMES--

--BEFORE *CUTTER* COMES DOWN FROM THE MOUNTAIN! IT'S A HARDER PLACE TO *LEAVE* THAN TO ENTER--AND GETTING IN IS HARD ENOUGH!

THOSE CURSED CARRION BIRDS WILL SHRED *ANYONE* WHO TRIES TO CLIMB UP TO THE AERIE.

GRRRR...

SCOUTER... CLEARBROOK... DEWSHINE...LITTLE WINDKIN... AND *CUTTER*, MY SOUL'S BROTHER--

--ALL INSIDE THAT *DUNGHILL!* YOU WOLVES SAY THEY LIVE...

BUT ARE THEY HIDING...? FIGHTING...? CAPTURED...?

"IF ONLY I COULD KNOW!" *SKYWISE* GROWLS, REMEMBERING HOW HE FOUND HIS TRIBEMATES' MOUNTS PROWLING IN THE TALL SHRUBBERY AT THE FOOT OF THE MOUNTAIN.

IT WAS AGONY TO RESIST THE TEMPTATION TO SEND, BUT *SKYWISE* DARED NOT RISK HIS MENTAL CALL BEING DETECTED BY *WINNOWILL*--FOR THEN SHE WOULD KNOW--

--IF SHE DID NOT ALREADY, THAT *MORE* WOLFRIDERS HAD SECRETLY ENTERED HER STRONGHOLD.

--HAD DEFINITELY *NOT* BELIEVED!

RUM TUM! RUM TUM! RUMMA-TUMMA TUM!

THERE GO THE DRUMS AGAIN. :SIGH: ANGRY HUMANS ARE ALL WE NEED NOW!

COME ON, *STARJUMPER*, BACK TO THE HOLT. WE'LL TELL THE OTHERS WHAT'S HAPPENED--

SO *SKYWISE* WAITED, LISTENING TO THE QUARRELS OF THE DIVIDED HOAN G'TAY SHO. SOME OF THEM, IT *SEEMED*, HAD BELIEVED *CUTTER* AND *NONNA'S* WARNING ABOUT *WINNOWILL*--WHILE OTHERS--

"--AND HOPE THAT, UNTIL WE CAN ALL COME AND HELP, *CUTTER* WILL SOMEHOW KEEP THINGS IN HAND."

PSSST!

IT'S SAFE. COME ON.

⟨*NONNA*, THIS PLACE IS NOTHING LIKE YOUR TRIBE SAID IT WAS!⟩

⟨THE OLD SONGS AND STORIES YOU TAUGHT ME--⟩

⟨--DO NOT TELL OF THINGS AS THEY ARE! OH, *ADAR*, MY HEART HURTS!⟩

⟨WHERE IS THE *MUSIC?* WHERE ARE THE *CLOUDS* LINING SOFT NESTS MADE OF SUNLIGHT?⟩

⟨HUSH, HUMANS! THE *EIGHT* HAVE HUNTERS' EARS!⟩

IT HAS NOT BEEN DIFFICULT FOR *CUTTER* AND HIS ODDLY ASSORTED BAND TO SLIP UNDISCOVERED DOWN THE DARK, ECHOING PASSAGES WITHIN BLUE MOUNTAIN. ALTHOUGH CONSTANTLY ON THE ALERT FOR A SURPRISE ATTACK, THEY HAVE SEEN NO MOVEMENT, HEARD NO SOUND SAVE THE SETTLING OF ANCIENT ROCK AND THE MINDLESS DRIP OF SEEPING WATER.

NOW AND THEN A FAINT, FAMILIAR SCENT TEASES...

DEWSHINE CAME THIS WAY-- BUT WHEN? HER TRAIL CROSSES AND RECROSSES ITSELF!

POOR HUMANS. THEY'RE SCARED-- AND DISAPPOINTED.

AND WHY NOT? WONDERFUL AS IT IS, THE PALACE OF THE *HIGH ONES* WASN'T AS MY MIND PICTURED IT, EITHER. ARE ALL LEGENDS JUST WIND?

10

12

OH, MY CUBS...!

YOUR LITTLE RIBS...! THEY *STARVED* YOU!

WE'LL MAKE THEM PAY!

THE SWEET, ELFIN LANGUAGE IS BEYOND *NONNA* AND *ADAR'S* KEN, BUT THE TEARS ARE ALL TOO EASILY UNDERSTOOD.

〈ADAR--〉

〈--WHERE IS THEIR BABY?〉

W-WINDKIN...?

SHE HAS HIM...ALWAYS! ...CARRIES HIM ABOUT LIKE A *DOLL!*

I THINK SHE'S DOWN BELOW IN HER DEN, NOW... I'M AFRAID 〈SOB〉 I-I'M AFRAID--

--SHE'LL *CHANGE* OUR CUB!

〈WHY DO YOU LOOK AT *ME,* SPIRIT?〉

〈WHAT DO YOU THINK OF THIS PLACE, *ADAR?*〉

〈IT IS *FOUL!* AND SO ARE THE SPIRITS WHO MADE IT!〉

〈THERE ARE HUMAN SLAVES HERE, REMEMBER?〉

〈WANT TO DO SOMETHING ABOUT IT...?〉

QUICKLY, WHEN THEY HAVE LEARNED THE WHEREABOUTS OF THE EIGHT FROM *DEWSHINE*...

〈ALL THIS *DARK*--ALL THIS *SICKNESS* BECAUSE OF THIS--THIS BLACK-ROBED ONE?〉

〈WHY DO WE NOT *KILL* HER?〉

UH...

〈KILLING SPIRITS IS VERY BAD MAGIC FOR HUMANS-- *BELIEVE* ME!〉

〈IT IS AS I SAID: WE MUST BREAK HER *POWER!*〉

"⟨AND TO DO THAT,⟩" CUTTER WHISPERS IN THE DIFFICULT HUMAN TONGUE, "⟨WE MUST FIRST GET RID OF HER WARRIORS!⟩"

⟨THERE THEY ARE...ALL TOGETHER... FEEDING!⟩

HEE HEE!

⟨GOOD! I'LL--⟩

⟨--PUT AWAY THAT SPEAR! WE MUST TRICK THEM --CATCH THEM OFF GUARD, THEN SNARE THEM IN OUR LITTLE WINGED FRIENDS' WEBS!⟩

CUTTER EXPLAINS HIS FULL PLAN TO A SKEPTICAL ADAR.

⟨HMM...YOU KNOW, SPIRIT, YOUR FIRST IDEA, TO TALK TO NONNA'S TRIBE--

⟨--DID NOT GO SO WELL. ARE YOU SURE ABOUT THIS?⟩

⟨I AM SURE I CAN TRUST YOU TO DO YOUR BEST! NOT EVEN SPIRITS ARE PERFECT. ASK YOUR CHIEF, OLBAR, SOMETIME. HE'LL TELL YOU.⟩

⟨AND ADAR... MY NAME IS --⟩ CUTTER. ⟨CAN YOU SAY IT?⟩

⧽GRFL PLTZ⧼

SHORTLY...

WHAT IS THIS?!

ONE OF OUR LORD'S PETS HAS GOT-TEN OUT OF ITS CAGE!

NONSENSE! SHE WOULD NEVER PERMIT IT! SHE HAS SENT HIM TO US.

OF COURSE! WINNOWILL HAS REALIZED THAT SHE HAS BEEN NEGLECTING US OF LATE.

⧽HEH-HEH⧼ THOSE WHO SERVE MUST SOMETIMES BE SERVED!

THE LITTLE SPIRIT WITH THE TONGUE-TANGLING NAME SAID THIS SOUR JUICE WILL MAKE THESE BIRD-RIDERS DROWSY.

THEY SEEM TO LIKE IT WELL ENOUGH!

SO, HUMAN...HAS OUR LORD WHISPERED HER SECRETS TO YOU? WHAT OF THE EGG? WHEN WILL SHE AWAKEN THE SLEEPERS?

UUHH...

HMMM...A QUIET ONE! HE KNOWS NOT EVEN ONE OF OUR WORDS.

STRANGE...

:COUGH:

I--I CANNOT BELIEVE IT! OUR LORD WILL NOT COME!

NO? WELL, WHATEVER HER REASONS, THANK THE **HIGH ONES!**

HAUGH! :KOFF: :KOFF:

FINALLY **WINNOWILL'S** WEB IS BEGINNING TO SAG. THOUGH WE HAVEN'T DONE IT NEATLY, WE HAVE CUT A FEW THREADS--

"--AND SHE'S HELPING US TO SLASH **MORE** RIGHT NOW!"

DOWN IN THE INNER ROOTS OF BLUE MOUNTAIN ARE LUXURIOUS ROOMS THAT EVEN THE EIGHT ARE NOT ALLOWED TO VISIT--

--ROOMS THAT NOW SEEM DINGY AND UNKEMPT, FOR THE HUMANS WHO ONCE TENDED THEM HAVE BEEN SHUT AWAY.

NO, MY CHOSEN, I WILL **NOT** SAVE YOU FROM THIS NEWEST HUMILIATION. IF ONE SLIP OF A WOLFRIDER--

--AND A NEGLIGIBLE FLIGHT OF PRESERVERS CAN SO CONFOUND YOU, THEN THE SHAME IS MORE **MINE** THAN YOURS!

ONCE MORE, AND FOR THE LAST TIME, **BRING** ME THE **PRESERVERS!**

KAKUK AND HIS FELLOW CAPTIVES KNOW WHEN THEIR MISTRESS IS SENDING, FOR THE CHILL SILENCE GROWS MOMENTARILY MORE OPPRESSIVE.

MUMM? MLIH...?

16

17

THE SURPRISE WOULD, IN FACT, BE *CUTTER'S*, WERE HE PRIVY TO THE ONE-SIDED CONVERSATION TAKING PLACE IN HIS GREAT ENEMY'S CHAMBER.

SHE WHO BORE YOU IS MAKING AS MUCH TROUBLE AS SHE CAN.

INDEED, MUCH OF YOUR BRAVERY COMES FROM *DEWSHINE*.

BUT THIS... THE FLOATING ...IS YOUR TRUE SIRE'S GIFT TO YOU.

WERE YOU FULLY A WOLFRIDER AND NOT PARTLY THE PRODUCT OF *TYLDAK'S* WHOLESOME SEED--

--YOU WOULD NOT HAVE SURVIVED THE WORK I HAVE DONE ON YOU.

BUT MORE THAN THE TWO WHO JOINED TO GIVE YOU LIFE--

--I HAVE GIVEN YOU *TIME*. ALL TIME. YOU HAVE TAKEN MY MILK...AND I HAVE CLEANSED THE DEADLY WOLF BLOOD FROM YOUR VEINS.

YOU WILL LIVE *FOREVER* AND SEE THE FULFILLMENT OF A WISH I WAS FORCED TO SET ASIDE--

--BECAUSE MY POOR, CONSCIENCE-RIDDEN *VOLL* COULD NOT SHARE IT.

SO QUIET!

IF ONLY YOU WOULD LAUGH WITH JOY!

YOU ARE *PURE ELF* NOW--

--PURE...! N-NO!

18

WINNOWILL SHAKES HER SHINING MANE UNTIL WINDKIN'S FACE APPEARS AS HIS OWN AGAIN.

IT WAS AN ERROR!

A *GRAVE* ERROR! I CONFESS IT!

THAT IS WHAT COMES OF GOING *OUTSIDE* TO FIND WHAT HAS LAIN *WITHIN* ALL THE WHILE.

IT WAS THERE IN THE *EGG*--THERE FOR *ALL* TO SEE IF THEY HAD THE MINDS TO LOOK!

"BUT NO ONE GAZED AS *LONG* AS I DID--FROM THE CREATION OF THE VERY FIRST SHELL."

"THE GLIDERS HAD THEIR OWN CONCERNS BUILDING...SHAPING *BLUE MOUNTAIN.*"

"THEY WERE ALL SO SAFE--JUST AS *VOLL* WANTED--THAT THEY NO LONGER NEEDED THEIR HEALER."

"A GIFT CAN FESTER, YOU KNOW, TURN IN UPON ITSELF, WHEN NO ONE ELSE HAS USE FOR IT."

"BUT I DID NOT LET THAT HAPPEN TO ME! I EXPLORED--

--MEDITATED UPON THE *EGG*--"

--BUT THEY REFUSED ME..! I SHOWED THEM HOW TERRIBLE IT COULD BE *NOT* TO GROW! AND THEY PREFERRED *THAT!*

MMBLE!

RRRUUU

AH! HEAR...?

GASP! FEEL?

"--UNTIL I SAW THE MONUMENTAL JOKE WE HAD PLAYED ON OURSELVES --

I SHOWED THEM HOW TO GROW--"

NOW WE WILL BE--

--WHAT WE WERE *MEANT* TO BE ALL ALONG!

YOU SEE, *AROREE?* ONLY THE POWERS OF THE GLIDERS--

--CAN BRING THE PALACE BACK TO LIFE! YOU WANT THAT, DON'T YOU?

I-I WANT...TO THINK FOR MYSELF! *YES!* THAT IS WHAT I WANT!

EVERYONE *USES* EVERYONE! *NO ONE* TELLS THE WHOLE TRUTH!

GO, RAYEK! THE WOLFRIDERS LIVE IN THOSE WOODS! GO TO THEM! I WILL *NOT* FLY YOU ANY CLOSER TO BLUE MOUNTAIN!

DULLARD! CHILD-THIEF! BUT PERHAPS THIS IS FOR THE BEST, AFTER ALL--

--LEETAH IS HERE!

AS *RAYEK* GLIDES TOWARD THE EDGE OF THE FORBIDDEN GROVE HIS AIR OF COCKSURENESS GIVES WAY TO UNEASE--

--AND WONDERMENT. NEARLY ALL HIS TRAVELING TO THE FROZEN MOUNTAINS WAS DONE UNDERGROUND.

UNTIL NOW HE HAS NOT TRULY SEEN OR SCENTED THE GREEN GROWING PLACE--OR HEARD ITS MANY VOICES CALLING, FACELESS, IN THE DARK.

THE WOLVES ANNOUNCE THE COMING OF BLOOD WHICH THEY HAVE SMELLED BEFORE. THE WOLFRIDERS, WITH SENSES ONLY SLIGHTLY MORE KEEN, ALLOW *RAYEK* TO APPROACH THE FATHER TREE IN THE HEART OF THE GROVE.

HEY, BROWNSKIN! HOW FARE THE *GO-BACKS*? THEY KILLED ANY TROLLS LATELY? HOW MANY LITTLE BEAR-STABBERS ARE ON THE WAY--OR FAWNED ALREADY?

RAYEK CASTS A WITHERING GLANCE AT *KRIM*, THE GO-BACK TURNED FOREST-DWELLER. BUT HIS FEATURES SOFTEN AT THE SIGHT OF THE ONLY FACE THAT INTERESTS HIM--THE ONLY EYES THAT MEET HIS WITH LOVE AND FELLOW-FEELING.

LEETAH...

MY FRIEND! MY EYES SEE WITH JOY!

SOFTPRETTY HIGH-THING! HELLO! HELLO!

≷GIGGLE≷ *PETALWING*! YOU'RE HERE *TOO*!

SUCH A *SHORT* WHILE IT HAS BEEN SINCE WE LAST TOUCHED! IF ONLY THE TIME OF THIS MEETING WERE HAPPIER!

HAVING LEARNED ENOUGH FROM *SKYWISE*, THROUGH *ARORE*, TO HAVE FORMED HIS OWN ARCH OPINION OF RECENT EVENTS, *RAYEK* SMILES.

EEP!

I SEE SOFT LIVING HAS MADE YOU WOLFRIDERS LOSE YOUR NERVE, ELSE WHY HAVE YOU NOT CONFRONTED *WINNOWILL* OPENLY? YOU HAVE ALREADY PROVED THAT SHE CAN BE BEATEN!

SMART WORDS AT LAST--AND IT TOOK A MUCKING MAGIC-USER TO SPEAK 'EM OUT!

SMART WORDS BORN OF-- FORGIVE ME--*IGNORANCE!*

IN OUR LAST ENCOUNTER WITH *WINNOWILL* WE PROVED *NOTHING!*

SHE DEFEATED *HERSELF!*

AYE! *KILLING* HER WOULD BE THE *EASY* PART!

--BUT THEN *YOU'D* HAVE HER RAGING *SOUL* TO DEAL WITH IN THE CASTLE, BLACK-HAIR--

"--AFTER SHE GOT THROUGH WITH *US!*"

THERE IS ONLY ONE WAY TO TEACH YOU WHAT WE ARE UP AGAINST, DEAR FRIEND.

SUNTOP, STRONGBOW AND I--

--*MUST SHOW* YOU!

NOW!

UUHHH...!

H-HIGH ONES! ENOUGH...! *ENOUGH!!*

B-BY THE SPIRITS OF ALL WHO DIED SINCE THE CASTLE FELL...! SHE MIGHT HAVE BEEN *MORE* THAN *TIMMAIN...!*

AAH! MY HEAD STILL *POUNDS!* TO HAVE SUCH GIFTS...AND YET LET THEM SLOWLY STARVE...FEEDING ONLY ON BITTERNESS... AND *PAIN...!*

23

24

JUST THEN...

WHUF!

≈WHINE≈
≈WHINE≈

AAYOOOAH!!

SKYWISE'S CRY BRINGS THE WOLFPACK'S LEADER LOPING UP TO GREET HIM.

HULLO, BRIERSTING!

GROWF!

AFTER A FEW QUICK HUGS AND HEARTY LICKINGS--

--THE STARGAZER ONCE AGAIN ACTS AS TIDINGS-BEARER TO HIS APPREHENSIVE TRIBEFOLK.

...AND AS FAR AS I KNOW CUTTER AND THE OTHERS ARE WELL.

BUT, FOR WHATEVER REASON, THEY HAVEN'T YET ESCAPED FROM THE MOUNTAIN.

CUTTER DID MANAGE TO STIR UP THE HUMANS. THOUGH NOT ALL OF THEM DOUBT THE "BIRD SPIRITS," SOME HAVE BURRS UNDER THEIR TAILS NOW!

POOR PLANNING YIELDS POOR RESULTS. AS USUAL YOUR CHIEF RELIES TOO MUCH ON CHANCE. "MAYBE THE HUMANS WILL TURN AGAINST WINNOWILL." "MAYBE WE CAN TRADE PRESERVERS FOR THE GIRL AND HER BABY."

EVERY EFFORT HE HAS MADE, SO FAR, HAS HAD NO TRULY USEFUL EFFECT.

AND NOW HE HAS GOTTEN HIMSELF AND TWO MORE OF YOU TRAPPED! GOOD LEADERSHIP INDEED!

25

YOU...!

YOU ALWAYS TURN UP WITH A SNARL AND A GLARE AND A MOUTH FULL OF WRONG-TAILED SCRUB ABOUT YOUR OLD RIVAL! IT STILL STINGS, DOESN'T IT, *RAYEK*?

BEING MASTER OF THE PALACE HASN'T CHANGED YOU MUCH AT ALL!

AT LEAST I AM MASTER OF SOME-THING, *SKYWISE*. YOU HAVE NOT EVEN MASTERED *YOURSELF*!

WAS IT NOT YOUR CARE-LESS RUTTING AFTER THE DULL-WITTED *AROREE* THAT PLACED YOUR TRIBE IN ITS PRESENT DIFFICULTY?

ANTS TAKE YOUR EYES!

THE VERY OBJECTS OF *SKYWISE'S* OATH NOW BLAZE WITH AMBER FIRE--A FIRE WHICH *FREEZES*, RATHER THAN BURNS.

C-CAN'T *MOVE*...!

THE WOLVES WATCH WITH INTEREST, ABIDING BY THE AGE-OLD LAW OF THE "STARE-DOWN." THEY DO NOT INTERFERE.

SKYWISE'S FIST TREMBLES IN MID-SWING, BUT THE BLOW CANNOT BE DELIVERED!

IMPATIENTLY, TREESTUMP INTERVENES.

BACK OFF, BOTH OF YOU! ALL THAT MATTERS IS THE *TRUTH*!

AND THE TRUTH IS, IT'S NOT *WINNOWILL'S* STRENGTH GETTING EATEN UP LITTLE BY LITTLE--IT'S *OURS*!

THERE'S BEEN TOO MUCH RUNNING ALONE--OUTSIDE THE PACK--HERE!

26

CUTTER WENT OFF AND LEFT ME TO SPEAK FOR HIM *BEFORE* ANY OF THIS TROUBLE STARTED. I GUESS HE'S DONE HIS BEST TO ROLL WITH THE BLOWS SINCE.

BUT AS ACTING CHIEF, I SAY *RAYEK'S* MADE *ONE* POINT.

WE'RE *NOT* HELPLESS! THERE ARE FOUR AMONG US, NOW, WHO CAN STAND UP TO THE BLACK SNAKE'S MAGIC--AND THREE OF THEM HAVE ALREADY BEEN TESTED!

IT'S UP TO *ME* TO DECIDE HOW TO USE THEM!

I KNOW *CUTTER* WOULD GIVE UP HIS LIFE TO KEEP FRIEND--

--OR LIFEMATE--

--OR CUB--

--FROM SUFFERING *WINNOWILL'S* TORTURES. BUT THAT SHE-SPIDER CAN'T DO EVERY-THING AT ONCE.

IF SHE IS BUSY KEEPING THE GLIDERS ASLEEP, AND IF SHE *IS*--HIGH ONES HELP THEM--PLAYING HER PAIN-GAMES WITH THE FIVE OF US SHE'S GOT NOW, HER MIND'S ON *THEM*, NOT ON US!

THE TIME IS RIGHT AND WE HAVE THE RIGHT WEAPONS! WE'RE GOING TO BLUE MOUNTAIN!

TAM... LIFEMATE...

THIS JOINING OF LIVES, ALL FROM SEPARATE PATHS--

28

SIEGE AT BLUE MOUNTAIN

ARTIST/WRITER
WENDY PINI

CO-PLOT/EDITOR
RICHARD PINI

PART 6

INKS
JOE STATON

LETTERER
JANICE CHIANG

WELCOME, *SAVAH*. TAKE CARE. THE WIND RISES WITH THE SUN.

MY FOOTING IS FIRM. BESIDES, THERE IS NO REST FOR ME BELOW.

I WILL STAND WITH YOU, *SUN TOUCHER*--

--AND FEEL THE WIND. DO *THEY* FEEL IT, TOO? IS IT HARSH OR GENTLE ON THEIR YOUNG FACES?

THEY MUST TAKE IT AS IT COMES, MOTHER OF MEMORY.

DART'S RIDERS MUST FACE THE STORM--GO THROUGH IT--ELSE THEY SHOULD NEVER HAVE LEFT THE SAFETY OF SORROW'S END.

THAT SAME MOMENT, FAR AWAY...

AS DAWNLIGHT PAINTS STRIPES OF GOLD ACROSS THE TOWERING CLIFFSIDE, HAGGARD ELFIN TRAVELERS THINK OF THE COOL UNDERGROUND CHAMBERS BENEATH THEIR HUTS--PLACES OF SHELTER FROM THE MIDDAY HEAT-- SHELTER WHICH NOW LIES DAYS BEHIND THEM.

SOON THE BLAZING DAYSTAR WILL SWEEP NIGHT'S LINGERING CHILL FROM THE SAND. THE JACK-WOLFRIDERS HASTEN TO PITCH THEIR TENTS.

WE WON'T CAMP HERE ALL DAY-- 'SOON AS THE HIGH WALL'S SHADOW IS LONG ENOUGH TO TRAVEL IN, WE'LL GO.

AYOOOAH! DART! LOOK AT THIS!

SOMEONE HAS SCRATCHED A SYMBOL INTO THE ROCK HERE...! LOOKS LIKE--

--THREE BEADS AND THREE CLAWS...

RAYEK! HE ALWAYS WORE THEM AROUND HIS NECK, REMEMBER?

I THINK I DO! HE LEFT THE SUN VILLAGE WHEN NEWSTAR AND I WERE JUST SMALL CUBS, DIDN'T HE?

HEY! WHAT'S THIS UNDER THE SAND...?

BITS OF BONE!

HOW DID THEY GET THERE?

AND WHO MARKED THE CAVE WITH A SYMBOL, AS IF IT WERE A-A BURIAL PLACE!?

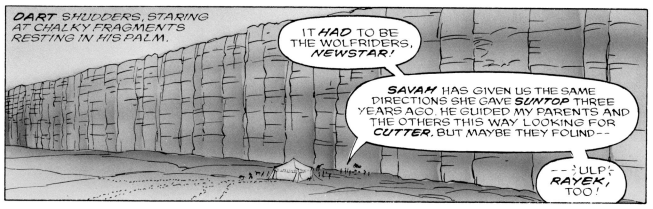

DART SHUDDERS, STARING AT CHALKY FRAGMENTS RESTING IN HIS PALM.

IT *HAD* TO BE THE WOLFRIDERS, *NEWSTAR!*

SAVAH HAS GIVEN US THE SAME DIRECTIONS SHE GAVE *SUNTOP* THREE YEARS AGO. HE GUIDED MY PARENTS AND THE OTHERS THIS WAY LOOKING FOR *CUTTER,* BUT MAYBE THEY FOUND--

--*ULP!* *RAYEK,* TOO!

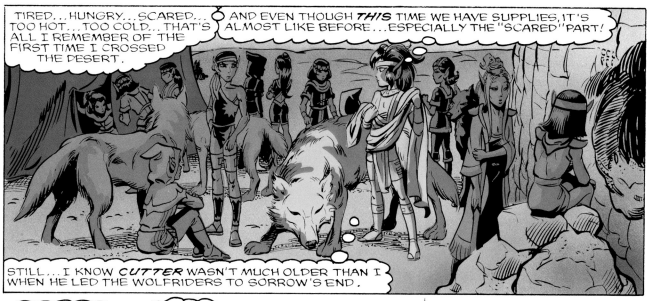

TIRED...HUNGRY...SCARED...TOO HOT...TOO COLD...THAT'S ALL I REMEMBER OF THE FIRST TIME I CROSSED THE DESERT.

AND EVEN THOUGH *THIS* TIME WE HAVE SUPPLIES, IT'S ALMOST LIKE BEFORE...ESPECIALLY THE "SCARED" PART!

STILL...I KNOW *CUTTER* WASN'T MUCH OLDER THAN I WHEN HE LED THE WOLFRIDERS TO SORROW'S END.

I CAN BE LIKE HIM--AND LIKE MY PARENTS, TOO!

THE WOLFRIDERS NEED HELP AND I WON'T STOP 'TIL I BRING IT TO THEM!

THAT EVENING...

COME, *LEETAH! BRIERSTING* WILL CARRY YOU AND *SUNTOP!* WE CAN GET THERE BEFORE SUNRISE! *HURRY!*

WE GOING *BIG BLUE ROCKS!* GET *FLYYYGH BABY!*

31

‡SOB‡ ‡SOB‡ --BUT-BUT I TOOK THE BLAME! I MADE SUNTOP "GO OUT" AND-AND I KNOW IT WAS WRONG!

‡SNIFF‡ PLEASE LET ME GO WITH YOU, PLEEEZE!

THROUGH THAT WEAKNESS I CAN REACH HER... *HEAL* HER! MY PRECIOUS ONE, I WOULD RATHER HAVE SUNTOP STAY HERE WITH YOU.

BUT WE *NEED* HIS GIFTS.

OH, CUBLING! YOU ARE NOT BEING PUNISHED! THIS TIME SOMETHING *GOOD* CAME OF YOUR DISOBEDIENCE. WE KNOW, BECAUSE SUNTOP TOUCHED HER SPIRIT, THAT WINNOWILL IS STRAINING HER POWERS.

IT IS TIME FOR HIM TO USE THEM.

AND...

‡SNIFF‡ WHEN WILL IT BE *MY* TIME, *REDLANCE?* ARE ONLY MAGIC-USERS USEFUL?

BEFORE MY POWERS AWOKE, CUB, *I* CRIED THOSE QUESTIONS *MANY* TIMES.

SO WHAT'S THE BIG WHOOP? DON'T TELL ME THAT *KAHVI* NEVER WENT OFF AND LEFT *YOU* TO GUARD THE GO-BACKS' LODGE!

THAT WAS *KAHVI!*

SHE KNEW US INSIDE OUT! IT JUST CHIPS THE POINTS OFF MY RACK THE WAY WE GET *BABIED* AROUND HERE!

PUCKERNUTS! I WANTED TO GO *BEAT* THOSE FLEA-FEAST GLIDERS!

DON'T THINK OF FIGHTING AS FUN YOU MIGHT BE MISSING, *EMBER.* ESPECIALLY NOT *MAGIC* FIGHTING.

SUNTOP IS SAFER GUARDED BY *RAYEK, STRONGBOW* AND *LEETAH* THAN HE WOULD BE IF HE'D STAYED HERE--

--WHERE WINNOWILL COULD STEAL HIS SPIRIT.

I... GUESS SO.

BESIDES, UNTIL *CUTTER* AND THE OTHERS COME HOME, *YOU* MUST BE, CHIEF! WHERE SHALL I GROW THE THORN FENCES AND STRANGLEWEED TRAPS TO KEEP ENEMIES OUT OF OUR HOLT?

;GIGGLE; *HUM!* I'LL HAVE TO THINK ABOUT THAT!

THEN I'LL JUST STAND RIGHT HERE AND AWAIT YOUR ORDERS!

EMBER IS *CUTTER* REBORN. IT'S AS IF THE SEASONS HAD TURNED BACK SO WE MIGHT SEE HIM AS A CUB AGAIN.

THE ONLY THING *SHE* FEARS IS GETTING CAUGHT IN A MISTAKE.

I WOULD NOT BE A CHIEF...

I WOULD NOT *WISH* TO BE SO WATCHED--OR ALWAYS FEEL THAT I MUST WATCH MYSELF!

AS *NIGHTFALL* GAZES FONDLY AT HER *LIFEMATE*, HIS SOUL NAME RIPPLES THROUGH HER MIND...

ULM--

"--HE'S TURNED OUR TROUBLES INTO A *GAME!*

WOOPS!

AW, *CHOP-LICKER!* YOU *STONEHEAD!* YOU'VE WRECKED THE TRAP!

SNAP!

WE'LL MEND IT, LITTLE CHIEFTESS. STRANGLEWEED DOESN'T DIE WHEN YOU BREAK IT, IT JUST GROWS ITSELF RIGHT BACK.

MAY ONLY FOUR-LEGGED THINGS COME TO TEST YOUR TRAPS, BELOVED...

AND, PLEASE--

⟨STOP, STRANGE ONES! COME NO CLOSER! WE HAVE STRONG MAGIC — *WEAPONS* GIVEN TO US BY THE *BIRD SPIRITS!*⟩

⟨YOUR WAY OF SAYING OUR WORDS IS HARD TO UNDERSTAND. WE MEAN NO HARM.⟩

TO MAKE HIMSELF CLEARER, THE SPEAKER BEGINS TO SIGN AS HE TALKS. THE OTHER MAN IS INCAPABLE OF SIGNING.

⟨WE SEARCH FOR AN EVIL SPIRIT WITH HAIR LIKE FROST — AND WHEN WE FIND IT—⟩

⟨—WE WILL KILL IT!⟩

⟨WE ARE CHILDREN OF *GOTARA,* THE MASTER SPIRIT. WE COME FROM THE FLATLANDS BEYOND THE DARK WOODS TO THE EAST. WE HAVE BEEN WANDERERS, BUT NOW WE ARE *SEEKERS.*⟩

⟨AH! THE FOUR-FINGERED ONES! THE WOLF-EYED ONES! WE HUNT THEM, TOO!⟩

⟨WE WERE ABLE TO NET THE DEMON BECAUSE HIS WOLF WAS LAME AND COULD NOT OUTRUN OUR PONY. BUT HE ESCAPED AND CUT OFF *BRUGA'S* FINGERS.⟩

⟨IF YOU WILL HAVE US, WE WILL JOIN YOU, FOR IT SEEMS WE ALL WANT THE SAME THING.⟩

AND SO, WITH THE BARRIER OF ACCENT AND DIALECT BREACHED, THE MEN UNITE IN PURSUIT OF THEIR COMMON QUARRY.

ONLY THE BOY, *GEOKI*, SHOWS NO ENTHUSIASM AS THE HUNT RESUMES.

NOW ALL IS MOVEMENT AND PURPOSE IN THE NORMALLY PEACEFUL VALLEY OF ENDLESS SLEEP--

--AS THREE DETERMINED GROUPS, TWO ELFIN--AND ONE HUMAN-- HURRY TOWARD THEIR GOALS.

LATER THAT NIGHT...

NOW THAT WE ARE SO NEAR BLUE MOUNTAIN, I FEEL--

--I *FEAR*--I WAS TOO HASTY. *LEETAH* SHOULD NOT HAVE TO CROSS WILLS WITH THAT SICK PAIN-GIVER, AGAIN--

--AND NEITHER SHOULD HER LITTLE SON.

I KNOW *WINNOWILL* SHE WILL LOSE ALL INTEREST IN HER CAPTIVES--

--IF I GIVE HER SOMETHING *NEW* TO FEED ON--

36

"--APPROVAL! THERE IS NOTHING WRONG WITH HER DESIRES--"

"-- ONLY WITH HER METHODS. WHEN SHE KNOWS SHE IS LONGER ALONE -- "

"-- HER PAIN WILL END."

WHY THAT PUFFED-UP DESERT RAT! HE'S TAKEN OFF ON HIS OWN!

BUT I-I THOUGHT THE PLAN WAS SET.

OH, RAYEK! HE MISLED US!

SMALL LOSS!

WE STILL HAVE ALL THE STRENGTH WE NEED!

SOON...

THE GREAT HAWKS ARE LETTING ME PASS. THEY TAKE ME FOR A GLIDER.

PUH! WHAT A STENCH OF DROPPINGS.

A STAIRWAY!

NOW, WHY IN YUREK'S NAME WOULD THE GLIDERS HAVE NEED OF... STAIRS?

PANT PANT HIGH ONES! I AM *DONE!* NEED TO REST.

EH...? WHAT IS THAT...THAT RUMBLING I HEAR?

STAY WITH ME, *PETALWING...*

YOU ARE MY ONLY GUIDE... IN THIS... DECAYING HIVE...

PETALWING STAY, *SHARPDARK HIGHTHING!*

SOME TIME LATER, NEAR THE CHAMBER OF THE GREAT EGG...

SILENCE, MY CHOSEN! SILENCE YOUR FEAR-ADDLED THOUGHTS!

I CANNOT FIND ANY *ONE* OF YOU IF YOU CONTINUE TO CALL ME ALL AT ONCE.

NO USE! SENDING CLEARLY THROUGH PRESERVER WEBBING IS TOO MUCH FOR THEM.

THAT FILTHY WOLFRIDER, *DEWSHINE!* THIS IS *HER* DOING!

AND NOW, OF *ALL* TIMES!

SHE CANNOT HAVE HIDDEN THE CHOSEN EIGHT BY HERSELF! IF SHE HAS MANAGED TO BRING ALLIES INSIDE MY MOUNTAIN--

--I *WILL* KNOW IT!

'LREE...! 'LREE...!

BUT JUST AS *WINNOWILL* USES *DEWSHINE'S* SOUL NAME TO FORCE HER OUT OF HIDING...

WINNOWILL! I AM RAYEK! MASTER OF THE PALACE OF THE HIGH ONES!

IT IS TIME WE MET!

LR--!?

IN *VOLL'S* NAME, WHAT *NOW?*

OOOOHH...!

WHO KNOWS? *RAYEK* AND *WINNOWILL*...HUH! NOW THERE'S A MEETING THAT WILL RATTLE THIS MOUNTAIN EVEN MORE THAN IT'S SHAKING NOW!

DEWSHINE!

IT-IT'S OVER....! SHE STOPPED!

AN OPEN SENDING! *RAYEK* IS HERE!

YES! DO YOU THINK HE'S COME TO HELP US?

...RRRUMMRRRRRUUMMMBLERRRUUM...

WHAT'S HAPPENING, BELOVED, DO YOU KNOW?

TYLDAK SAID...SOMETHING ABOUT...THE *EGG!* CUTTER, MY CUB! MY CUB!

YES, LITTLE COUSIN. *WINNOWILL'S* SCENT IS FRESH HERE. I THINK SHE CAME UP JUST A SHORT WHILE AGO.

-SNIFF SNIFF-

I...CAN'T TELL IF SHE HAD *WINDKIN* WITH HER...

...SOMETHING'S *STRANGE!*

< I DO NOT UNDERSTAND ALL THIS SPIRIT CHATTER! >

< WHEN DO WE FREE THE *SLAVES* YOU SAY ARE DOWN THERE? >

< RIGHT NOW, *ADAR!* >

WE'LL SEE IF *WINNOWILL* LEFT *WINDKIN* BELOW IN HER DEN. MEANTIME, YOU TRACK HER, *CLEARBROOK.*

AND FIND OUT WHAT *RAYEK'S* UP TO-- BUT DO NOTHING 'TIL WE JOIN YOU!

AYE, *CUTTER!*

WHAT OF THIS NEW INTRUDER, *RAYEK*? AMBITION POWER AND *NEED* ARE ALL IN HIS SENDING.

HIS WILL ENJOYS LUSTY HEALTH. BUT THERE IS SOMETHING HE WANTS--

--FROM *ME!*

"SUCH A NATURE I HAVE DEALT WITH BEFORE."

"IN ELF, HUMAN OR TROLL, WHERE *NEED* IS PRESENT, *CONTROL* IS SIMPLE."

"LEARN WHAT HE WANTS MOST AND GIVE IT TO HIM."

"THEN CREATE ANOTHER NEED AND FULFILL *THAT!*"

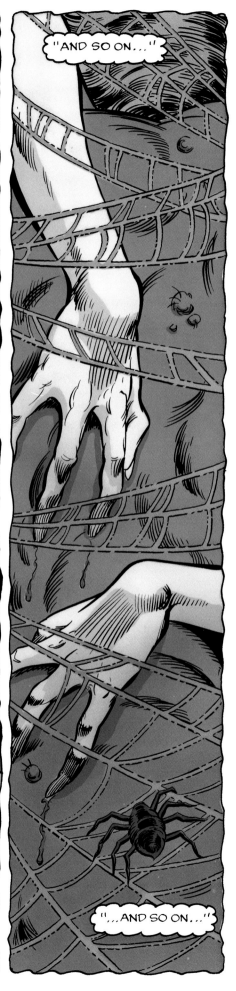

"AND SO ON..."

"...AND SO ON..."

"THERE IS BEAUTY IN NEED, IT IS *LIFE* TO A HEALER."

"BUT IN GREED WAITS BETRAYAL AND MANY FORMS OF DEATH."

THIS *RAYEK* AND HIS ESTIMABLE POWERS--

RECOGNITION? NO, THIS IS NOT--

--THE UNION OF TWO SOULS TO GIVE LIFE AND BREATH TO A THIRD.

--THERE IS ONLY ONE SOUL HERE, *RAYEK*--

--SHARED BY TWO FORMS, YOURS AND MINE--

--YOU KNOW THIS--

--AS DO I.

MEANWHILE, *CUTTER* CAUTIONS *NONNA* AND *ADAR*...

‹REMEMBER, HUMANS, NO MATTER WHAT, DO NOT TOUCH THESE ROUND THINGS!›

‹HOW CAN SOMETHING MADE OF *STONE* BURST LIKE A NUT HEATED IN A FIRE?!›

‹IT COULD MEAN OUR LIVES!›

BUBBLEBANGS!

‹YOU QUESTION TOO MUCH, *ADAR!* TRUST!›

‹WITHOUT THESE LITTLE ONES WE WOULD BE *LOST* IN THE GREAT CAVE OF SPIRITS!›

‹*HMPH!* WITHOUT THESE LITTLE ONES WE WOULD BE *HOME* INSTEAD OF HERE!›

‹SHHH! *WINNOWILL'S* CHAMBERS!›

WINDKIN ISN'T HERE... -CHOKE- HE ISN'T HERE!

44

<NONNA! LOOK!>

<OH...! CRUEL-- CRUEL TO DO!>

NAN...NAN IROEEN SEENDALTHERI...? UH... HUM... -COUGH-

-GASP- SO **STRANGE** TO HEAR **HUMANS** SPEAK OUR WORDS!

<KAKUK...! IS IT **YOU**?>

THE SKELETAL PRISONER BLINKS TWICE, BARELY COMPREHENDING HIS NATIVE LANGUAGE...

THEN...

<WH-WHERE IS SHE?>

IN RESPONSE, ADAR TURNS...

<DO NOT WORRY ABOUT THAT BLACK CROW!>

<SHE WILL NOT HARM YOU--

<--EVER AGAIN!!>

KA-KRAK!

45

<WHAT NOW? HOW DO WE GET OUT OF HERE?>

<WE CAME IN THROUGH A DOOR MADE OF MOVING ROCK. CAN YOU MAKE THE ROCKS OPEN AGAIN, LITTLE SPIRIT?>

<YOU *STILL* HAVE FAITH?>

<I STILL *LOVE*.>

SCOUTER, DEWSHINE, TAKE THE HUMANS TO THE AERIE. THEY'LL HAVE TO CLIMB DOWN THE MOUNTAIN FROM THERE... SOMEHOW. HELP THEM.

BUT--

DON'T WORRY. WITH *CLEARBROOK'S* AID AND *RAYEK'S*, IF HE'S STILL A FRIEND, I'LL GET *WINDKIN!*

THEN... YOU STILL PLAN TO DO--

--WHAT I DID ONCE BEFORE: LOCK MINDS WITH THE BLACK SNAKE-- MAKE HER FORGET *EVERYTHING* BUT HER NEED TO KILL *ME!*

NO MATTER WHAT HAPPENS--

--YOUR *CUB* WILL BE BACK IN YOUR ARMS, *DEWSHINE,* SOON!

AT THAT MOMENT IN THE FORBIDDEN GROVE...

OOOOWWW OOOOOOOOWWWOO OOOOOO WWWOO

HUMANS!

THEY'RE COMING THIS WAY, UP FROM THE WINDING RIVER!

ARE THEY THE HOAN G'TAY SHO?

DO THEY COME IN PEACE...?

THE INNOCENT HOPE IN *REDLANCE'S* SENDING SOON FADES, FOR--

--AS THE WAR PARTY APPROACHES THE HOLT, THE ELVES SENSE THE HUMANS' HOSTILE INTENT.

〈HEAR THE HOWLING OF THE WOLVES!〉

〈HAH! THEY ARE WITH THEIR DEMON RIDERS IN THE WOOD OF DREAMS!〉

〈REMEMBER, THE EVIL ONES' SIZE MEANS NOTHING. LIKE *ANTS*, THEY ARE MUCH STRONGER THAN THEY LOOK.〉

〈BUT *WE* CAN CRUSH THEM, EVEN SO!〉

DON'T LOOK SO WORRIED, *REDLANCE*. THIS'LL BE FUN! ALL OUR TRICKS AND TRAPS ARE READY AND THE PRESERVERS ARE *FULL* OF SPIT!

GRRUFF!

HOW MANY ARE THERE, BELOVED?

TWICE OUR NUMBER, PLUS TWO WHO RIDE A *NOHUMP*.

NOHUMP?

LATER!

WHY SEND? WHAT'S TO FEAR? IF *THOSE* ARE HUMANS, THEIR ARMS AND LEGS AREN'T *HALF* AS BIG AROUND AS A TROLL'S! *LET* THEM HEAR US LAUGH!

HUSH, SKOT!

48

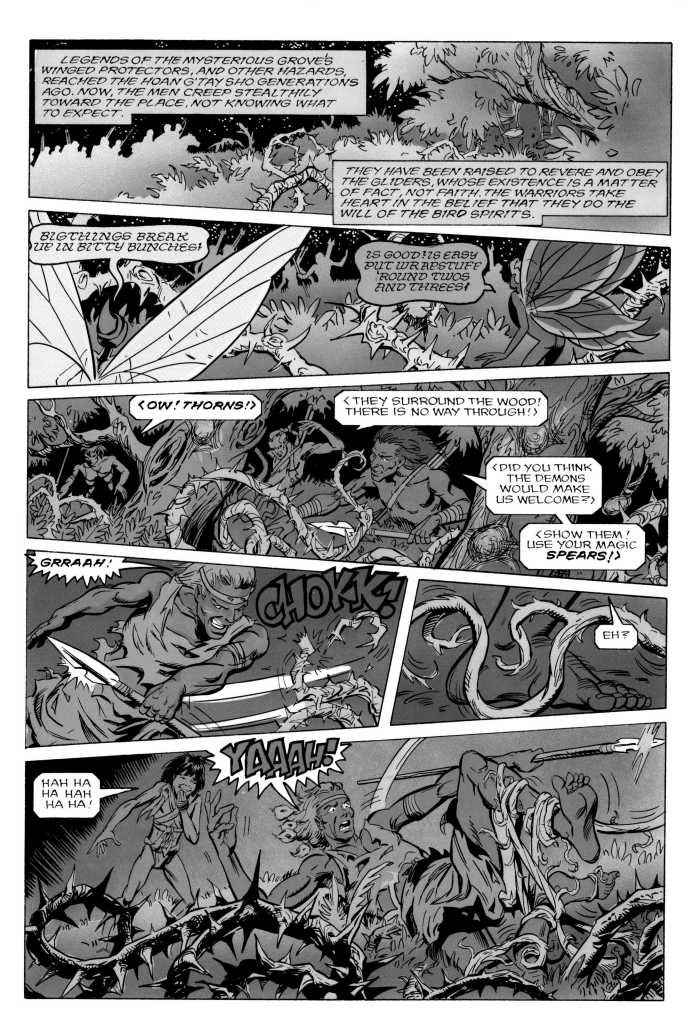

SNAP!

52

GREAT SUN! HUMANS!

DON'T BE AFRAID!

SURROUND THEM!!

DART! BY BY THE HIGH ONES AND ALL THEIR CHILDREN!

DART!!

AAYOOAH!

UNH! NOT SO HARD, EMBER!

LOOK AT YOU! BROWN AND BEAUTIFUL AS LEETAH-- AND TALLER THAN YOUR FATHER!

~SIGH~ IF STRONGBOW AND MOONSHADE WERE HERE...

REMEMBER ME?

NEWSTAR! I REMEMBER A *LITTLE* CUB, SHY AND FRAGILE AS A NEWGREEN BUD--

--NOT A *MAIDEN*, TALL AND GOLDEN AS A SUNFLOWER!

WE CAME BECAUSE OF *SUNTOP* AND WHAT *SAVAH* LEARNED FROM HIM.

WHILE THE HUMANS LOOK ON, SOME WITH LOATHING, MOST WITH FEAR, THE ELVES COMMUNICATE THROUGH *SENDING* ALL THAT HAS HAPPENED SINCE *WINNOKIN* WAS STOLEN.

AND WHEN *DART* HAS LEARNED ALL...

EVEN WHEN I WAS A CUB, I DIDN'T BELIEVE HUMANS WERE *ALL* BAD. I STILL DON'T. *THESE* ARE HERE BECAUSE OF THIS--THIS *WINNOWILL* CREATURE, SHE'S LIKE NO ELF I EVER HEARD OF!

AMONG THE GLUM FACES IN THE CAPTIVE WAR PARTY, *DART* SEES ONE WHOSE SMILE HE GENTLY RETURNS...

...FOR YOUTH KNOWS A BROTHER OF ITS OWN HEART AND HOPE--NO MATTER WHAT PHYSICAL DIFFERENCES EXIST.

DART HAS COME BACK TO THE GREEN GROWING PLACE WHERE HE SPENT HIS EARLIEST YEARS.

BUT HE HAS COME AT A TIME OF GREAT TROUBLE FOR THE WOLFRIDERS, AND HIS OWN PACK OF DESERT-BORN HUNTERS ARE FRIGHTENED BY HIS LAND'S STRANGENESS.

DART GAZES AT THE DISTANT MOONLIT PEAK OF BLUE MOUNTAIN AND WONDERS... WILL HE BE ANY HELP AT ALL?

TO BE CONTINUED...

SIEGE AT BLUE MOUNTAIN

ARTIST/WRITER
WENDY PINI

CO-PLOT / EDITOR
RICHARD PINI

PART **7**

INKS
JOE STATON

LETTERER
JANICE CHIANG

LORD VOLL'S HIGH-BACKED CHAIR STANDS EMPTY AT THE HEAD OF A BARREN TABLE. WHEN SHE LAST SAW IT, *CLEARBROOK* RECALLS, THE DINING CHAMBER GLOWED WARMLY WITH THE LIGHT OF MANY CANDLES, AND STRANGE, DELICIOUS MEATS WERE SERVED ON SHINING PLATTERS.

BUT THAT WAS THREE TURNS OF THE SEASONS AGO WHEN *VOLL* LIVED AND STILL HELD SOME SWAY WITHIN BLUE MOUNTAIN.

PRESERVER WEBS, CUPS AND TRAYS SCATTERED EVERY-WHERE! THE CHOSEN EIGHT PUT UP MORE OF A FIGHT THAN *CUTTER* AND *ADAR* BRAGGED!

NO MATTER! I'M GLAD THOSE GUARDS ARE OUT OF THE WAY. *WINNOWILL* IS ENOUGH TO DEAL WITH. ÷ MUNCH ÷ I'D BEST GET BACK ON HER TRAIL.

CLEARBROOK DELAYS BUT A MOMENT LONGER TO TUCK A FEW MORSELS INSIDE HER BELT POUCH. THEN SHE IS OFF DOWN ANOTHER DARK HALLWAY--

--FOLLOWING WINNOWILL'S DELICATE-BUT-RECENT SCENT TO THE THRONE ROOM, WHERE...

TYLDAK!

¿OOHHH...?

Y-YOU HAVE A WEAPON...? GOOD!

USE IT!

I AM SICK,... AND WEARY.

YOU'RE FAINT WITH HUNGER. HERE. EAT. BY TIMMORN'S BLOOD! THE BLACK SNAKE CAN MAKE ME PITY ANYONE--

--HUMANS,... GLIDERS...EVEN YOU, WHO LEFT ME AND MINE TO THE TROLLS THAT KILLED MY LIFEMATE!

¿UUNNNH!? STUPID! WHAT MADE ME THINK I COULD BUDGE YOUR CHAIN!?

TELL ME WHERE IS WINNOWILL NOW?

IN THE CHAMBER OF THE GREAT EGG--

--WITH THE STRANGER, RAYEK!

58

UNABLE TO DO ANYTHING MORE FOR *TYLDAK*, AND PRICKED BY HIS WORDS, *CLEARBROOK* DASHES OFF--

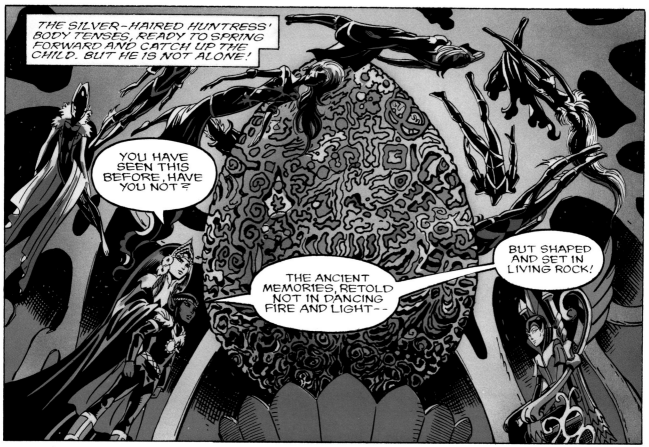

59

A **STONE** SCROLL OF COLORS!

YES! YOU PRIDE YOURSELF ON HAVING UNEARTHED OUR RACE'S BEGINNINGS.

BUT YOU SEE...YOU NEED NOT HAVE GONE AS FAR AS THE PALACE OF THE HIGH ONES.

IT WAS **HERE**, ALL THE WHILE--A TRUTH NEEDLESS OF REDISCOVERY, FOR IT WAS NEVER FORGOTTEN.

NOT, AT LEAST, BY **ME**.

YOU ARE WRONG, BEAUTIFUL MASK.

THE TRUTH IS NOT **ALL** HERE.

¿CHUCKLE¿ DEAR SOUL OF MINE, I THOUGHT YOU MORE OBSERVANT! THERE IS **MORE** TO THE **EGG**!

LOOK! **SEE**!

SPIRIT OF OROLIN!

I **DO** SEE!

?

IT HAS BEEN MY SOLE AND CONSTANT OCCUPATION SINCE **VOLL** DIED. MY LONG-DELAYED TASK IS NEARLY ACCOMPLISHED.

YOU WILL MAKE THE FINISH EASIER FOR ME.

EVER SO GENTLY THE BLACK SNAKE ENTWINES HER PREY.

WILL YOU NOT SHARE THE BURDEN...EVEN AS YOU SHARE THE VISION?

¿GASP¿-I-I MEANT TO **WIN** THE GLIDERS TO MY CAUSE...NOT TO **CONTROL** THEM, AS YOU HAVE DONE.

THE STARS BECKON, **RAYEK**...

60

NO! YOUR PEOPLE'S HEARTS ARE NOT IN IT!

AND NEITHER IS THEIR FULL POWER, YOU *KNOW* THAT!

THEY CANNOT RESIST THE TWO OF US.

RAYEK...

NOW THAT *YOU* ARE WITH ME--

--NO MORE WAITING--

--THERE WILL BE NO MORE WITHHOLDING--

--AND, ONCE WE ARE FREE OF THIS TWICE-CURSED WORLD, *NO MORE* MISTAKES!

UNDER M--*OUR* GUIDANCE THERE WILL NEVER BE ANOTHER "ACCIDENT" AS THAT WHICH EXILED THE FIRST COMERS HERE, WEAK AND ALL BUT DEFENSELESS.

BUT...THE PALACE--!

--IS NECESSARY! IT IS PART OF THE POWER WE NEED. WE WILL TAKE IT WITH US--

--BUT THE JOURNEY BEGINS WITH THE EGG!

CLEARBROOK STRUGGLES TO HOLD DOWN THE SLIGHT NOURISHMENT SHE TOOK A SHORT WHILE AGO.

SHE HAS NEVER DREAMED OF, MUCH LESS WITNESSED, SUCH A VIOLATION-- SUCH CALLOUS MANIPULATION OF ANOTHER'S NEEDS AND WEAKNESSES.

MEANWHILE, IN TENSPAN'S HALL...

〈ADAR, C-COULD I NOT WAIT AND USE THE FOOT-HOLDS?〉

〈HEH...WOULD I HAVE COME THIS FAR TO DROP YOU *NOW*, WOMAN?〉

LISTEN, LITTLE COUSIN. THESE HUMANS HAVE BEEN MISTREATED. THEY'RE WEAK. IF IT LOOKS LIKE THEY CAN'T MAKE IT DOWN THE MOUNTAIN FROM THE AERIE, JUST WAIT FOR ME.

WE'LL THINK OF SOMETHING.

I'M THINKING OF *STRONGBOW*. HE COULD GET "DOOR" TO OPEN.

OH, *CUTTER*, I KNOW YOU'VE STOOD UP TO *WINNOWILL* BEFORE-- BUT IF SHE GETS AT YOUR *SOUL*, SHE-SHE...FORGIVE ME! GOOD HUNT, MY CHIEF!

THAT'S WHAT I NEED TO HEAR, *DEWSHINE*.

AND *YOU*...!

LET'S SEE A *SMILE*! GOOD HUNT, *CUTTER*!

SOON...

〈FOLLOW, HUMANS! *THIS* WAY!〉

〈*PANT PANT*: THE CHILD SPIRITS RUN LIKE THE GREAT BIRDS FLY!〉

〈TOO *GASP* SWIFTLY!〉

WE MAKE ROPES FOR CLIMBDOWN!

SPOOT

HEE HEE!

GO, *BERRYBUZZ*! FLY OUTSIDE AND FIND US THE EASIEST WAY DOWN! AND *DON'T* GET EATEN BY GIANT HAWKS!

IN A SHORT WHILE...

〈IT IS NOT MUCH FARTHER. DO NOT FEAR.〉

SCOUTER IS SURPRISED BY HIS OWN CONCERN FOR "TALL ONES". THE LONGER HE IS WITH THEM, THE LESS THREATENING THEY SEEM.

〈THERE *NONNA*!〉

〈THAT IS WHERE WE HID ONE OF THE BIRD RIDERS!〉

AND...

RAAWK?

RRUMMBLE!

HMMM... ANYPLACE NOT SO GOOD FOR CLIMB DOWN!

TOO MUCH SHAKY~ SHAKE!

OOPS!

NOSY OUTSIDE BIGTHINGS HEAR SHAKY~ SHAKE, TOO!

EEYIPE!

GROWLER HIGHTHINGS!

WHY FOR EVERYBODY COME~GO COME~GO?

SHOULD JUST STAY HOME SAFE! SHOULD!!

HELLO! HELLO!

OH!

BERRYBUZZ! TELL US WHAT'S HAPPENED! WINDKIN...! CUTTER...! DEWSHINE...! TALK!

WHEN ONE ASKS A PRESERVER TO TALK, ONE DOES SO ADVISEDLY!

...THEN BIG BLUE ROCKS GO SHAKY-SHAKE AND WE LET LOOSE BIGTHINGS FROM CAGE...

...AND WE PUT WRAPSTUFF 'ROUND BAD FLYTHINGS, THEN PUT BAD FLYTHINGS IN HIDEY-HOLES...

...AND SHARPDARK HIGHTHING COME, THEN SHINYSWORD HIGHTHING SAY GO BY SELF, FIGHT BAD LONGSOFT-HAIR HIGHTHING GET FLYHIGHBABY BACK...

...AND LOOKSEE! LOOKSEE! MANY BIG-THINGS GUARD DOOR!

HUNH! I BET THEY'D SOONER FEED US TO THE GIANT BIRDS THAN BOW AND SCRAPE AS THEY ONCE DID FOR CUTTER, EH, STRONGBOW?

DEJECTEDLY, THE ARCHER NODS.

BUT WE HAVE TO GET IN--

--BEFORE CUTTER FACES WINNOWILL! I'D RATHER SLASH MY WAY THROUGH EIGHT EIGHTS OF HUMANS THAN LET HER EVEN BREATHE ON HIM!

SHH...SKYWISE, THERE IS ANOTHER DOOR, REMEMBER? IN WINNOWILL'S PRIVATE CHAMBERS.

SUNTOP CAN FIND IT FOR US.

LEETAH'S CALM ASSURANCE COOLS THE STARGAZER'S TEMPER.

IF ANYONE HAS A RIGHT TO WORRY ABOUT CUTTER, IT'S LEETAH. SHE DOESN'T BLAME ME FOR CAUSING THIS MESS--

--SO I'D BEST STOP BLAMING MYSELF, AND DO WHATEVER I CAN WITHOUT BARKING.

WITH PAINSTAKING SLOWNESS, THE ELFIN BAND PICKS ITS WAY AROUND THE BASE OF BLUE MOUNTAIN. SUNTOP'S SPECIAL SENSE--HIS "MAGIC FEELING"--IS OPEN TO RECEIVE ANY TINGLING HINT OF DOOR THE ROCK-SHAPER'S PRESENCE.

OTHER SENSES, LUPINE ONES, ARE ALREADY DISTRACTED BY SOMETHING UNSEEN.

THE WOLVES... THEY KEEP LOOKING OFF TOWARD THE *HOLT!*

BUT BEFORE *STRONG-BOW* CAN WHISPER HIS CONCERN TO HIS COMPANIONS...

GOLDEN DESERT CHILD, YOU SEEK A WAY *IN.* LIKE MICE YOU SQUEAK--

OH, NO....!

--BECAUSE YOU CANNOT FIND YOUR HOLE!

GRRRR...

AND *THESE* ARE FINDERS OF THE *SCROLL!*

HAHAHAHAHA!

WHAT?! THE WINNERS OF THE *PALACE*--

--*LOST?* MOTHER HAS YOU TURNED AND TOSSED!

WITHOUT EXPRESSION, WITHOUT SO MUCH AS THE BLINK OF AN EYE, *STRONGBOW* DRAWS AND AIMS.

WAIT.

THIS OLD ENEMY DESERVES A *SPECIAL* REVENGE--

--ONE THAT I HAVE IN MIND FOR HIS *MOTHER* AS WELL, IF I EVER GET MY HANDS ON HER...!

66

LEETAH...?

SIGH CLOSE...! A MOMENT MORE --

--AND THE MADNESS WOULD HAVE LEFT HIM.

YOU CALLED THAT MONSTER "SON"! HOW *COULD* YOU?!

IT... WAS WHAT HE SEEMED TO NEED MOST!

TREESTUMP AND THE OTHERS CATCH UP WITH SKYWISE AND SUNTOP...

HURRY! COME LOOK! WE LOST TWO-EDGE --

BUT SEE WHAT WE FOUND!

A SECRET DOOR, HIDDEN BY THE BUSHES! WE'VE SEEN ITS LIKE BEFORE, EH?

TWO-EDGE'S SCENT IS STRONG THROUGH HERE!

AND THE OTHER "DOOR" ELF IS NEAR! HE JUST OPENED AT THE END OF THIS TUNNEL!

WELL, YOU WON'T BE NEEDING THAT BOW OF YOURS, STRONGBOW.

"BERRYBUZZ SAID THE ONLY ONE IN THE MOUNTAIN LEFT FOR US TO DEAL WITH IS WINNOWILL --"

"--AND, OF ALL CURSED THINGS, IT'S UP TO US KEEP HER *ALIVE*!"

RRRRRUUM...

RRRRUMMMBLE...

RRRRUMM...

67

TO *BE* AS A *HIGH ONE...* WOULD THAT NOT SATISFY THE LONGING WHICH PAINS YOU MOST? THINK, MY SOUL'S BROTHER, WHAT IT WOULD MEAN TO BE *WHOLE*--

--TO HAVE A BODY OF YOUR OWN ENVISIONING--

--SHAPED FIRST BY ME... THEN, IN TIME *RESHAPED* AS OFTEN AS YOU WISHED BY *YOUR* WILL ALONE!

IT WOULD MEAN *REBIRTH,* NOT JUST FOR ME, BUT FOR *ALL* OUR KIND: WOLFRIDERS, SUN FOLK, GO-BACKS, EVEN ELVES YET TO BE DISCOVERED! THE BEINGS OF *FIRE* WE ONCE WERE -- WE CAN BE AGAIN!

AND THE FEW OF US WHO KNOW THE OLD POWERS--

--AND WHO HAVE GRIEVED AT BEING *CRIPPLED* IN THEIR USE--

--WILL GRIEVE NO MORE! EVEN *YOU,* A CONFUSION OF PLEASURE AND PAIN, *TIMMAIN'S* EQUAL CONFINED TOO LONG IN A DARKNESS WHICH HAS *UNHINGED* YOU--

--WILL BE WHOLE! ALL THE WRONG YOU'VE DONE WILL BE REMEMBERED ONLY AS A LESSON WELL-LEARNED.

MMM...

THE PREY IS DOWN!

THEN GO, *HIGH ONE-THAT-SHALL-BE*--

70

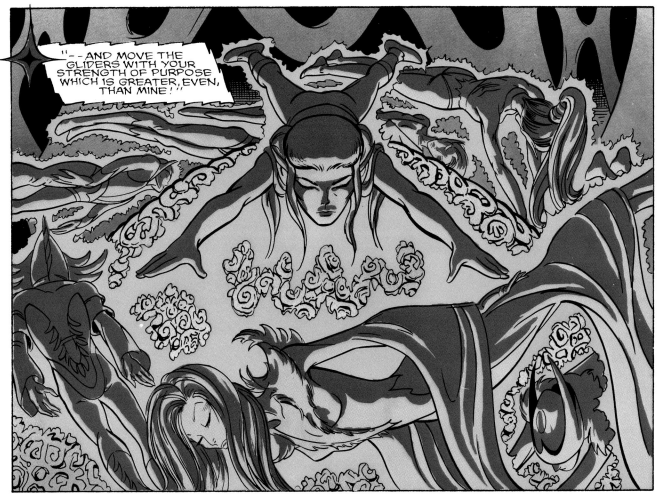

"--AND MOVE THE GLIDERS WITH YOUR STRENGTH OF PURPOSE WHICH IS GREATER, EVEN, THAN MINE!"

WATCHING WITH HORRIFIED FASCINATION, CLEARBROOK STARTS AS *CUTTER* APPROACHES AT A WOLF-SOFT RUN.

THEY NOD A QUICK GREETING, THEIR EYES SPEAK.

THEY KNOW THEIR CHANCE TO SNATCH THE CUB IS NOW--

--OR NEVER!

BUT...

⸮GASP!⸮

WHA--?!

BRUMBLE RRUMM!

CRRREEEEAK!

THE SHAPING FORCE THAT SURGES THROUGH EVERY NOOK AND CRANNY OF BLUE MOUNTAIN IS LESS POTENT NEAR WINNOWILL'S PRIVATE QUARTERS.

SUNTOP IS ABLE TO SENSE THE SECOND "DOOR'S" LOCATION—ON THE OTHER SIDE OF THE WALL AT THE TUNNEL'S END.

DOOR, OPEN! DOOR, OPEN!

STRONGBOW "LOCK-SENDS", HOPING THAT WINNOWILL IS TOO BUSY ELSEWHERE TO PIERCE HIS MENTAL SHIELD.

DOOR OPEN!!

DOOR, OPEN!!

HIS RECEPTIVITY MUDDLED BY THE GREAT UPHEAVAL, DOOR SHIFTS ON HIS SEAT.

HE HAS ALREADY PERFORMED FOR ONE HE KNOWS...

OPEN! OPEN! NOW!!

BUT THIS NEW COMMAND IS SENT BY AN INTRUDER—A STRONG ONE—

——TOO STRONG TO RESIST!

YES! OBEY ME! OPEN AND STAY OPEN!

HE DID IT! LEETAH, SUNTOP——

——GO!

BUT...

OH!

LOOK OUT!!

IT'S CLOSING AGAIN!

73

MOTHER...!

M-MY EYES SEE WITH JOY! MY HANDS... TOUCH...

FATHER...?

YOU... LOOK LIKE A THISTLE!

GIVE ME THE CUB.

HE IS NO LONGER YOURS.

STRANGE... YOUR SENDING WAS A *SHOCK* THE FIRST TIME I FELT IT. NOW IT SEEMS QUITE *TAME.*

I CAN AFFORD A SLIGHT DISTRACTION NOW, WITH *RAYEK* HELPING TO KEEP THE GLIDERS' ATTENTION ON THEIR TASK.

YOU REMEMBER *MY* SENDING--

--DO YOU NOT WOLFLING?

THE *CUB,* CLEARBROOK ...QUICK!!

CUTTER SHIVERS, MAKING NO SOUND.

BUT, FAR BELOW, HIS PAIN IS FELT, AND HIS SILENT CRY IS HEARD BY ONE WHOSE SOUL IS LINKED WITH HIS!

OH, *TAM!*

SUNTOP, DO NOT SEND TO *SKYWISE!* THERE IS STILL A CHANCE WE CAN TAKE *WINNOWILL* BY SURPRISE!

LEETAH IS FORCED TO MAKE A HEARTBREAKING DECISION!

MOTHER, WE *CAN'T* LEAVE HIM LIKE THAT!

AND WE CANNOT STOP *WINNOWILL* UNLESS I *TOUCH* HER!

IN THE BLACKNESS OF THE STONE POCKET WHICH ENCLOSES HIM, THE STARGAZER CAN ONLY GUESS AT WHAT IS HAPPENING.

HE, TOO, SHARES *CUTTER'S* SOUL NAME. HE, TOO, FEELS HIS FRIEND'S PAIN— MORE THAN HIS OWN FEAR.

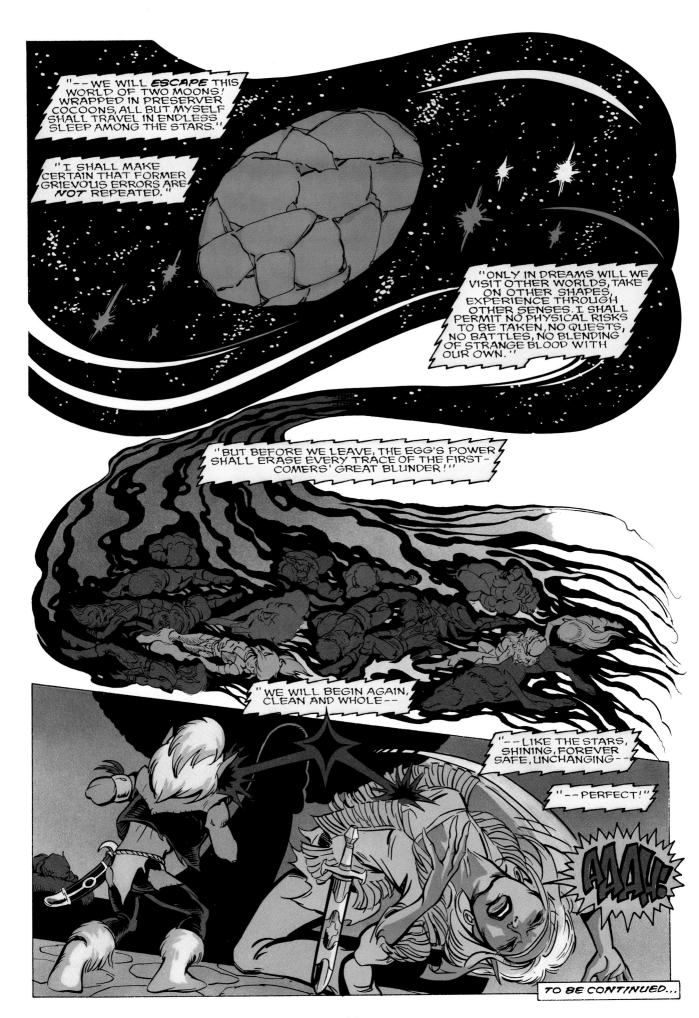

"--WE WILL *ESCAPE* THIS WORLD OF TWO MOONS! WRAPPED IN PRESERVER COCOONS, ALL BUT MYSELF SHALL TRAVEL IN ENDLESS SLEEP AMONG THE STARS."

"I SHALL MAKE CERTAIN THAT FORMER GRIEVOUS ERRORS ARE *NOT* REPEATED."

"ONLY IN DREAMS WILL WE VISIT OTHER WORLDS, TAKE ON OTHER SHAPES, EXPERIENCE THROUGH OTHER SENSES. I SHALL PERMIT NO PHYSICAL RISKS TO BE TAKEN, NO QUESTS, NO BATTLES, NO BLENDING OF STRANGE BLOOD WITH OUR OWN."

"BUT BEFORE WE LEAVE, THE EGG'S POWER SHALL ERASE EVERY TRACE OF THE FIRST-COMERS' GREAT BLUNDER!"

"WE WILL BEGIN AGAIN, CLEAN AND WHOLE--

"--LIKE THE STARS, SHINING, FOREVER SAFE, UNCHANGING--

"--PERFECT!"

AAAH!

TO BE CONTINUED...

84

SIEGE at BLUE MOUNTAIN

ARTIST / WRITER	CO-PLOT / EDITOR	PART	INKS	LETTERER
WENDY PINI	RICHARD PINI	8	JOE STATON	JANICE CHIANG

EVERYONE KNOWS THE AIR IS **ALWAYS** THERE BETWEEN THE WORLD AND THE STAR-HOLDING SKY. AIR CANNOT BE DRAINED LIKE WATER...IT CANNOT BURN ITSELF OUT LIKE FIRE... NO, THE AIR IS **ALWAYS** THERE--

¿GASP?

--JUST AS A MOUNTAIN THAT HAS STOOD FOR TIME UNTOLD--

IS ALWAYS THERE. SACRED MOUNTAINS DO NOT CHANGE INTO STUPENDOUS **EGGS**--

--AND AIR DOES NOT ABANDON ITS BREATHER--

--EXCEPT, IT SEEMS, ON THE WORLD OF **TWO MOONS** WHERE BOTH EVENTS ARE PERCEIVED AS--

--MAGIC!

SPIRIT MAGIC!! WE WILL DIE!!

WHILE THE TERRIFIED HUMANS COWER IN THE VAST SHADOW OF BLUE MOUNTAIN-THAT-WAS, *SKYWISE* FIGHTS FOR CONSCIOUSNESS IN HIS SEALED TOMB WITHIN THE EGG.

≥PANT≤
≥PANT≤

MY RIBS ACHE SO...!

WHY?

...IS IT SOME NEW PAIN-SENDING FROM *WINNOWILL?* NO! SHE'S FIGHTING *CUTTER* NOW...DOESN'T KNOW I'M HERE.

MY *ARM*..!

WANT TO BREAK SILENCE... SEND FOR HELP!

CAN'T! *LEETAH* MUST GET TO *CUTTER!*

IF IT'S HIM OR ME, SHE HAS TO HELP *HIM!*

HE *HAS* TO WIN, *HIGH ONES!* HE *HAS* TO!

AT THE SAME TIME...

THE INFANT LIES WITHIN REACH. THE INNOCENT ONE HAS BECOME THE PRIZE IN THIS DUEL BETWEEN CHIEF AND LORD.

THROUGH A RED HAZE OF PAIN, *CUTTER* SENSES HIS TRIBEMATE *CLEARBROOK*, HAS FALLEN.

BEAST-BLOODED *FOOL!* YOU ARE THE ONLY ONE OF YOUR KIND WITH STRENGTH ENOUGH TO SLAY ME. BUT KNOWLEDGE INHIBITS YOU.

BECAUSE YOU DARE NOT DESTROY *MY* BODY, I AM FREE TO DESTROY *YOURS* -- BY DEGREES!

AND YOUR SPIRIT, WOLFRIDER, THAT TOO WILL I KILL!

YOU AND YOUR TRIBE ARE *FINISHED!*

W-WINDKIN...! OOOHH...!

THE FLOORS NO LONGER HEAVE AS THEY DID MOMENTS AGO. WAVERING WALLS AND COLUMNS SETTLE INTO THE LACY PATTERNS THAT HELP TELL THE GREAT EGG'S EON-SPANNING TALE.

BUT *SUNTOP* AND *LEETAH*, ARRIVING AT ITS CORE, CARE NOTHING FOR THIS TWISTED STONE RECORD OF ELFIN LORE.

THEY SEE ONLY THE UNEQUAL BATTLE RAGING SILENTLY IN THE CHAMBER BEFORE THEM.

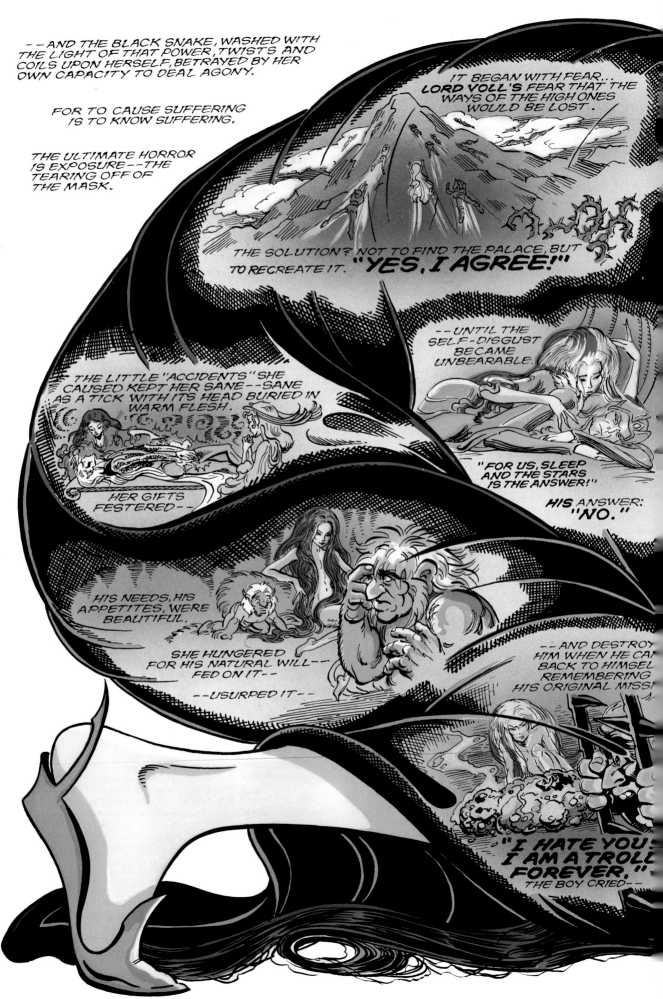

--AND THE BLACK SNAKE, WASHED WITH THE LIGHT OF THAT POWER, TWISTS AND COILS UPON HERSELF, BETRAYED BY HER OWN CAPACITY TO DEAL AGONY.

FOR TO CAUSE SUFFERING IS TO KNOW SUFFERING.

THE ULTIMATE HORROR IS EXPOSURE--THE TEARING OFF OF THE MASK.

IT BEGAN WITH FEAR... LORD VOLL'S FEAR THAT THE WAYS OF THE HIGH ONES WOULD BE LOST.

THE SOLUTION? NOT TO FIND THE PALACE, BUT TO RECREATE IT. "YES, I AGREE!"

--UNTIL THE SELF-DISGUST BECAME UNBEARABLE.

"FOR US, SLEEP AND THE STARS IS THE ANSWER!"

HIS ANSWER: "NO."

THE LITTLE "ACCIDENTS" SHE CAUSED KEPT HER SANE--SANE AS A TICK WITH ITS HEAD BURIED IN WARM FLESH.

HER GIFTS FESTERED--

HIS NEEDS, HIS APPETITES, WERE BEAUTIFUL.

SHE HUNGERED FOR HIS NATURAL WILL-- FED ON IT--

--USURPED IT--

--AND DESTROY HIM WHEN HE CAM BACK TO HIMSEL REMEMBERING HIS ORIGINAL MISSI

"I HATE YOU! I AM A TROLL FOREVER." THE BOY CRIED--

THE GLIDERS STOPPED DYING. STOPPED BIRTHING. "THEY DO NOT NEED ME!"

IN TIME, SHE DISCOVERED THE GREAT JEST -- THAT WORLDS DIE -- EVEN THE WORLD OF TWO MOONS.

REDEMPTION. SHE LEFT BLUE MOUNTAIN TO FIND THE TRUE PALACE -- FOR VOLL.

INSTEAD SHE FOUND A TROLL SENT BY GREYMUNG TO CAPTURE ROCK-SHAPERS.

--AND CRIED. HE WOULD HAVE GONE UP AND CRIED HIS OUTRAGE TO VOLL.

PROTECT VOLL. PROTECT SELF. THAT WAS WHY THE CAGE --

--AT FIRST, THEN THE GAMES BEGAN--

--MOTHER AGAINST SON.

SHE COULD NOT BREAK HIM. BUT SHE COULD SPLIT HIS MIND IN TWO!

THE FIRST TOUCH OF HEALING FORCES HER TO REMEMBER--

-- HER CHILD'S FACE AT THE VERY MOMENT SHE MADE HIM MAD!

RAYEK...! AS YOU LOVE ME... SAVE ME!

AGAIN...

ALMOST...

HE ALMOST FALLS UNDER HER SPELL...

BUT THE PITEOUS SOUND-MEMORY OF YOUNG TWO-EDGE'S SOBS BLENDS IN RAYEK'S MIND WITH THE WAILS OF HIS OWN BABE--THE NEWBORN THAT SOMEHOW HE KNOWS IS ALIVE!

RAYEK DRAWS BACK, REPULSED BY THE CHILD-HARMER.

DO I STILL DREAM? THE CRIES...!

SHE TRICKED ME, MOCKED ME... EVEN IN JOINING!

AAAAA AWAAAAA!

UUNHH... CUB!

SCOUTER'S CUB!

91

LIKE HUNTED GAME BACKED TO THE EDGE OF A CLIFF--

--WINNOWILL LAUNCHES A LAST FRENZIED ATTACK!

BUT SHE IS EXHAUSTED, AND *LEETAH'S* MINISTRATIONS HAVE BEGUN TO TAKE EFFECT. THE BLACK SNAKE'S BITE IS VENOMLESS.

THEY KNOW HER.

SHE CANNOT FIGHT.

SHE CANNOT HIDE.

STILL QUIET...! IS GOOD! *PETALWING* MAKE WRAPSTUFF!

AND...

I'LL CHASE YOU TO THE END OF THE WORLD, HALF-TROLL! LET THE CUB GO!

--TO KNOW EMOTIONS OTHER THAN CONFUSION AND HATE. BUT CLEARBROOK WOULD NOT LIKELY LISTEN.

HE UNDERSTANDS HER FURY. HE WOULD LIKE TO TELL HER SO.

IT FEELS SO GOOD--

HER HEART IS SET ON REVENGE. HE KNOWS HOW THAT IS--

--SO HE RUNS--

--THROUGH A MISSHAPEN OPENING WHICH WAS ONCE THE ENTRANCE TO THE GLIDER LORD'S THRONE ROOM.

THERE TWO-EDGE FINDS ANOTHER OF HIS MOTHER'S TOYS PUNISHED FOR DEFIANCE--LIKE HIMSELF-- ABANDONED.

YOU ARE HIS FATHER. TAKE HIM!

EH?

TAKE HIM!

WHAM!

TAKE HIM WHERE HE'S WANTED MOST!

BAH...?! BABAH...?

95

NONNA, THE SYMBOL MAKER, BREATHES A PRAYER, THEN FAINTS DEAD AWAY!

IT IS ONE THING TO HONOR THE GODS, BUT ANOTHER THING ALTOGETHER TO *FLY* WITH THEM!

THE FIVE HUMANS CANNOT *"SEND"* TO THEIR TRIBEFOLK BELOW, AS *SCOUTER* SENDS TO HIS--

--BUT HUMAN AND ELFIN ARMS BOTH ARE WAITING OUTSTRETCHED...

〈KAKUK!〉

GOT YOU, LAD!

AND SOON AFTERWARD, THE ASTOUNDED *HOAN G'TAY SHO* SEE *TYLDAK* UP CLOSE FOR THE FIRST TIME!

NOTHING--NEITHER FEAR FOR FRIENDS STILL TRAPPED WITHIN THE EGG, NOR THE WEIRD TANG OF LITTLE *WINDKIN'S* SCENT--MARS THE ECSTACY OF THIS REUNION. THE "NOW OF WOLF THOUGHT" ADMITS ONLY HAPPINESS--

--HOWEVER SHORT-LIVED IT MAY BE.

BE WELL, WOLFRIDERS!

DEW-SHINE! CUB!

I MUST RETURN TO *WINNOWILL,* THAT SHE MAY FEEL THE POWER--

--WAIT--!

--OF THE *TALONS* SHE GAVE ME!

98

IT IS MADNESS! OF ALL THE WOLFRIDERS, ONLY **STRONGBOW** HAS THE STRENGTH OF WILL TO MAKE BLUE MOUNTAIN'S STONE-STILL "DOORS" RESPOND.

--OR I'LL OPEN YOU!! AND YOU'LL BE AWAKE FOR IT-- --BELIEVE ME!

IN SENDING, THERE IS ONLY TRUTH.

THE SHEER BRUTALITY OF HIS TRUTH SURPRISES EVEN CUTTER.

HOWEVER--

:GASP:

:GASP:

--ONLY RESULTS MATTER!

SKYWISE!

:COUGH: :COUGH:--STARS! I'VE MISSED YOU...!

WITH THE CHAMBER CRUMBLING AROUND THEIR EARS, THE TWO FRIENDS REMAIN LOCKED IN A GRATEFUL BEAR-HUG. THEN-- REALIZATION!

HAVE TO ESCAPE!

BUT SKYWISE IS WEAK!

AND DOOR'S LEGS ARE LIMP AS WATER WEEDS.

HE'S FORGOTTEN HOW TO WALK--

BUT HE'S NOT A MUSHROOM! HE WANTS TO LIVE-- LIKE ANYONE ELSE.

CUTTER GRABS DOOR BY THE SCRUFF OF THE NECK, HAULING HIM-- AND SKYWISE-- INTO THE DARK, SEALED TUNNEL.

PRODDED BY CUTTER'S SENDING, DOOR BEGINS TO REMOVE THE FROZEN WAVES OF ROCK WHICH OBSTRUCT THE PASSAGE.

CRRREEAAK!

IT IS A RACE AGAINST DESTRUCTION AS THE TUNNEL CAVES IN BEHIND THEM!

AAH!

WORK FASTER, DOOR!

I SEE LIGHT!

AFTER DAYS OF CONFINEMENT IN THE OPPRESSIVE GLOOM OF BLUE MOUNTAIN, CUTTER BREATHES THE CLEAN, SUN-WARMED WIND THANKFULLY.

WE'RE OUT!

PRAISE THE HIGH ONES! IT'S ALMOST OV--

--ER...!

HELP...!

THERE YOU ARE, WOLFRIDER!

THERE WAS NO WAY BACK IN!

COME! I WILL LOWER YOU BOTH TO THE GROUND!

DOOR, TOO! WE CAN'T LEAVE HIM!

WHAT?!

NO! YOU OAF! I-I CANNOT! IT IS, TOO--

MMOUUUGH!

UUPF!!

THERE'S MY LAD! DON'T EVER GO OFF ON YOUR OWN AGAIN!

WE NEED A CHIEF--AND I DON'T LIKE THE CHORE!

SMAK!

FLUMP!

MOTHER!!

NO ...!

SHE... DIDN'T GET OUT! SHE...

SHATTERED, LIKE THEIR SACRED MOUNTAIN, LIKE ALL THEIR ANCIENT BELIEFS, THE HOAN G'TAY SHO BEAR THEIR LOSS QUIETLY. IT IS A LOSS TOO GREAT TO PROTEST.

THE DUST OF CATACLYSM SWIRLS, A BROWN, SUN-VEILING CLOUD SO ENORMOUS THAT IT SEEMS TO MAKE A **SOUND**--

--A LOW THUNDEROUS GROAN.

SHE ISN'T DEAD..... SHE ISN'T!

THAT MOTHERS AND FATHERS BOTH CAN PERISH UNTIMELY IS NO DELIBERATE INJUSTICE ON LIFE'S PART: **SCOUTER** KNOWS THAT LIFE IS JUST LIFE.

AND SO HE IS NOT QUITE ASTONISHED WHEN HIS SEND-CALL IS SWIFTLY ANSWERED.

MOTHER...? *PLEASE!*

I'M HERE, CUB!

THIS, TOO, IS JUST LIFE.

H-HOW DID YOU--?

IT WAS **TWO-EDGE**...! HE CAN **SEND** NOW, DID YOU KNOW THAT...? **LEETAH** MUST HAVE WORKED ON HIM.

HE MADE THE FEMALE *"DOOR"* OPEN FOR ME...

SAVED ME...

AND HIM- SELF?

I DON'T KNOW. I STABBED HIM... ONLY THEN DID HE SEND. I FELT... SAW... FORGAVE. BUT HE STAYED BEHIND.

103

FOR SOME, FORGIVENESS IS AS HARD TO FIND AS IS THE SUN BEHIND ITS DARK CURTAIN OF DUST.

‹DEMONS! -SOB'- THEY MOCK US IN THEIR VICTORY.›

‹THEY HAVE DESTROYED THE BLACK-ROBED MOTHER! DESTROYED THE BIRD SPIRITS' HOME!›

‹AND THERE THEY STAND, GLARING WITH THEIR EVIL EYES!›

‹MY FATHER... -SNIFF- THEIR EYES ARE JUST VERY BIG!›

‹I THINK...MAYBE... THEY ARE PEOPLE--›

‹--SPIRIT PEOPLE!›

I WISH I HAD WORKED HARDER AT LEARNING THE TALL ONES' WORDS.

DART HAS WON THAT YOUNG HUMAN'S HEART.

SEEMS SO.

RAYEK...?

YES... I SHALL!

?

‹GEOKI IS A FOOLISH BOY! IF THE DEMONS HAD NOT STOLEN OUR MAGIC SPEARS--›

CHINK

‹--WE EEEAAAGH!

YOU FAILED, HUMAN!

I WILL SHOW YOU HOW TO KILL HOWLING DOGS!

UUUUNNH...

KUREEL!

HA HA HA HAH HA!

THE INTENDED PREY IS SMALL AND FOUR-FINGERED.

BUT *KUREEL* IS A MINION OF THE *BLACK SNAKE*; HIS POISONOUS SOUL KNOWS DELIGHT AS RANDOM VICTIMS SCREAM AND DIE!

I'LL TURN THAT BIRD!

NO! THE ANGLE IS WRONG!

A TERRIBLE SHADOW FALLS OVER *GEOKI.* PETRIFIED, THE BOY CANNOT RUN.

GET DOWN!

WHIZZZ!

LITTLE STINGING WORM! WE'LL TEAR OFF YOUR *HEAD!*

GEOKI!!

WHOOOSH!!

AAAA!

RAYEK! WHY DON'T YOU--?!

KUREEL IS PLEASED. CHILDREN OF BOTH TRIBES WILL DIE NOW, IN PARTIAL ATONEMENT FOR HIS LORD *WINNOWILL'S* FALL--

--AND EVEN FOR HIS PITIFUL FOLK, THE *GLIDERS,* WHO LIE CRUSHED BENEATH THE RUINS OF AN OLD, OLD DREAM.

THOUGH THEY WOULD HAVE TAKEN HIM DOWN WITH THEM, HE WILL AVENGE THEM, TOO.

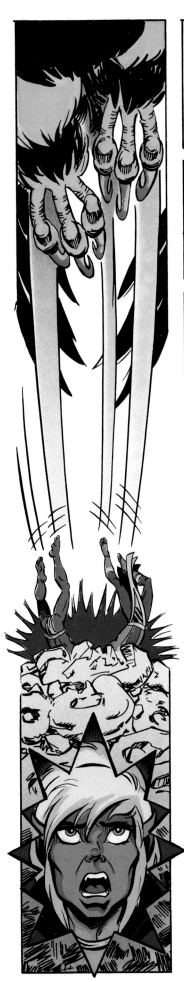

MAN KILLS MAN. IT IS THE WAY OF HUMANS.

BUT WITHIN THE COLLECTIVE MEMORY OF THE FOUR KNOWN TRIBES, ELF HAS *NEVER* KILLED ELF.

THE WORLD HAS CHANGED--

--AGAIN.

⟨GEOKI...! DO NOT BE DEAD!⟩

TH—THEIR HANDS! THEY WON'T COME APART!

GEOKI'S FATHER RECOILS, TRYING TO PULL HIS SON AWAY AS LEETAH HESITANTLY PLACES HER PALM ON THE SHATTERED BREAST.

THE DESTRUCTION OF AN ENTIRE MOUNTAIN DOES NOT MEAN SO MUCH AS ONE HOPED-FOR SHUDDER OF BREATH.

BUT IF SPIRITS THEMSELVES CAN DIE, TO WHAT POWER CAN PRAYERS BE OFFERED?

MOMENTS LATER, SHE IS UNITED WITH HUMAN AND ELFIN YOUTH——

——LOCKED, AS THE BOYS' HANDS ARE LOCKED, IN THE GRIP OF DEVOTION——

——TO LIFE!

SO MUCH TIME GOES BY THAT THE GREAT GRAY DUSTCLOUD DISPERSES.

THE SUN RETURNS.

UUNNNHHH...

AND...

TAM... I AM *LOST!* I-I THINK I WILL NEVER BE MYSELF AGAIN!

HUMANS... ARE SO-- SO *SET* IN THEIR MOLD!

THEN LOOK AT WHAT YOU *KNOW,* BELOVED--

"--LOOK AT WHAT YOU'VE DONE!"

FOR THE FIRST TIME -- IN HOW MANY DAYS, HE DOES NOT KNOW -- *CUTTER* REALIZES THAT HIS BODY IS NOT TENSED TO FIGHT OR FLEE. HIS FAMILY IS SAFE. HIS TRIBE IS REUNITED WITH KIN AND FRIENDS FROM FAR AWAY. ONLY ONE THOUGHT TROUBLES HIS HARD-WON PEACE.

WINNOWILL...! IF *TYLDAK* KILLS HER, HER SPIRIT WILL BE ON US LIKE A *PLAGUE!*

AND ALL THIS WILL HAVE BEEN FOR NOTHING!

DON'T WORRY. *TYLDAK* WOULDN'T DO ANYTHING TO HURT US. I KNOW HIM. I *TRUST* HIM.

DEWSHINE WISHES SHE COULD BE AS CERTAIN OF HER OWN CUB'S NATURE. THE BRIGHT-EYED BABE SHE CHERISHES MORE THAN LIFE ITSELF HAS BEEN TAMPERED WITH.

A WOLF-LING NO MORE... WHAT *IS* HE?

HMMHMM... POOR *GLIDERS!* BURIED ALIVE!

YES... *ALIVE!*

RAYEK! WHAT--?

THEY ARE ALL HERE... WITH *ME!* EVEN *KUREEL* REJOICES! *I* AM THEIR MOUNTAIN NOW...! *I* AM THEIR WAY TO THE *HIGH ONES'* HOME...!

¿GASP!¿

THEIR POWER BELONGS TO THE PALACE!

CLEARBROOK, LOOK AT HIS *EYES,* WILL YOU?! HE'S MANY NUTS SHY OF A FULL POUCH!

HE TELLS THE TRUTH! THE AIR IS *FULL* OF SOULS! BUT HE'S NOT FIT, AS HE IS, TO TRAVEL ALONE TO THE FROZEN MOUNTAINS.

THEN YOU AND I WILL TAKE HIM!

SOON...

‹NONNA...ADAR..., WE WILL REMEMBER YOU ALWAYS IN OUR HOWLS--THE FIRST HUMANS WE HAVE HONORED SO.›

‹NONE OF US WILL FORGET WHAT WE HAVE SEEN TODAY.›

‹I DO NOT KNOW WHY YOU HUMANS SET *US* SO HIGH ABOVE YOU. IT MAKES TOO MUCH FEELING... TOO MUCH HATE...TOO MUCH LOVE. *LEETAH* HAS PROVED THAT WE ARE MORE LIKE YOU THAN NOT.›

‹BUT IT IS HARDER TO LOSE BELIEFS THAT MAKE YOU FEEL SAFE--›

‹--THAN IT IS TO LOSE A *HOME!* I KNOW!›

‹TODAY, YOUR MAGIC--›

‹BUT IF WORSHIP DISPLEASES YOU--›

‹--BROUGHT DOWN BLUE MOUNTAIN AND HEALED ONE OF OUR OWN! I BELIEVE WHAT I *SEE.*›

‹--THEN TAKE FRIEND-SHIP!›

"‹ I WILL MAKE THE *HOAN G'TAY SHO* A SYMBOL--›"

"‹-- THAT WILL SPEAK TO THEM OF THE HEALING MAGIC. ›"

"‹ THEY WILL WALK IN THE WORLD KNOWING WHAT THEY KNOW: THAT SPIRITS CAN BE POWERFUL HELPERS WHO SOMETIMES NEED HELP TOO.›"

TWO NIGHTS LATER...

THE PRESERVERS ARE NOT HAPPY. FOR TWO LIGHTS AND TWO DARKS, THEIR PRECIOUS COCOONS HAVE BEEN TRIPPED OVER, DANCED ON, TANGLED AND TORN. SPLASHED DREAMBERRY JUICE DRIPS LIKE STICKY DEW FROM THE WINGED SPRITES' WEBS.

THE WOLVES, TOO, ARE NOT HAPPY. HACKLES ARE UP AND TAILS ARE BRISTLING OVER THE INTRUDING PACK FROM THE DESERT.

BUT NONE OF THAT DISTURBS SUNTOP AS HE COMMUNES SERENELY WITH SAVAH-- AND THEN SHYLY, REVERENTLY OFFERS HIS SPIRIT-HAND TO TIMMAIN, HERSELF.

EMBER, MEANWHILE, IS IN HER GLORY, ELABORATING YET AGAIN THE TERRORS AND TRIUMPHS OF HER GREAT BATTLE WITH THE HUMANS.

BUT THE SONG OF CELEBRATION, UNION AND REUNION HOLDS A PENSIVE NOTE FOR SOME.

AND FOR THE ONE WHO FOUGHT HARDEST TO PRESERVE "THE WAY"--YET, WITH AN ARROW, CHANGED HIS WORLD FOREVER--THERE IS NO SONG BUT SILENCE.

MY CUB...! I'LL NEVER KNOW HIM BY SCENT AGAIN! WHAT DID SHE DO TO HIM?

WHAT DOES IT MATTER? HE'S STILL OUR "BUMPER". AND WE ARE HIS ONLY PARENTS.

⁓GIGGLE!⁓

BA-BAH!

THERE!

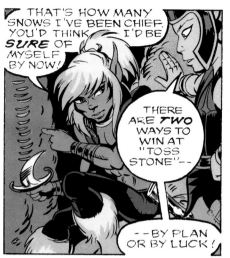

THAT'S HOW MANY SNOWS I'VE BEEN CHIEF. YOU'D THINK I'D BE *SURE* OF MYSELF BY NOW!

THERE ARE *TWO* WAYS TO WIN AT "TOSS STONE"--

--BY PLAN OR BY LUCK!

YOU PLAYED MOSTLY BY LUCK IN BLUE MOUNTAIN, BUT WHO CARES? YOU WON!

WHAT ABOUT *WINNOWILL?*

TRUST LUCK AGAIN! IT SEEMS TO *WORK* FOR YOU!

"AND SOMETIMES..." THINKS THE STARGAZER, *"BELIEVING THINGS WILL TURN OUT WELL IS THE ONLY THING WE CAN DO."*

CHIRR *CHIRR*

KRIK *KRIK* *KRIK*

HELLO ♪♫

OH...! *NEWSTAR!*

YOU SURELY GREW UP! THE SUN VILLAGE MUST *MISS* ITS PRETTIEST MAIDEN.

I LIKE IT HERE!

SNORT

AND I LIKE LOOKING AT THE STARS, TOO!

BUT DID YOU KNOW...YOU CAN SEE THEM *MUCH* BETTER--

--IF YOU LEAN BACK?

SIGH...

111

AND...

...STARS ARE SO BRIGHT. I CAN SEE THEM THROUGH THE LEAVES.

AND YOU KNOW... I LIKE 'EM RIGHT WHERE THEY ARE!

STRANGE HOW SOME OF US WOULD DO *ANYTHING* TO REACH THEM.

WHAT IS *FOR* US, DOES NOT PASS *BY* US, BELOVED.

THE GLIDERS NEVER WISHED TO BE PART OF THIS WORLD.

WHEN THEY WERE FREE, AT LAST, OF *WINNOWILL'S* CONTROL, THEY CHOSE TO EXIST ONLY IN SPIRIT.

I WOULDN'T! I *LIKE* HAVING SKIN.

THERE'S MY SKIN... AND THERE'S ME... AND WHEN I DIE ⸘YAWN⸘ THERE'LL STILL BE ME...!

BUT I'LL LET *THIS* WORLD DECIDE WHEN...! ZZZZ

NO!

HOW *EASY* IT WOULD BE TO BECOME LIKE *HER* --

-- TO DENY OTHERS THEIR CHOICES EXCEPT AS THEY SUIT *MY* DESIRES!

THE ONLY DIFFERENCE IS *LOVE,* HIGH ONES... KEEP ME STRONG!

AND BE WITH MY SUFFERING SISTER --

Gallery 6

In the Gallery for Volume Five of this series we mentioned that other, "side door" *Elfquest* stories had appeared from time to time. Following the cover artwork that showcased *Siege at Blue Mountain* issues 5 through 8, we present another such story. Entitled "Homespun," it first appeared in 1980 in the premier issue of *Epic Illustrated*, a magazine of adventure and fantasy published by Marvel Comics in an attempt to reach an older, more mature audience than the the one that traditionally buys comic books.

Invited to produce a story for that first issue, Wendy wanted to do an *Elfquest* tale, but knew that it had to (a) fit into only 8 pages and (b) stand on its own, since we couldn't assume that everyone who purchased *Epic* also read *Elfquest*. Thus, "Homespun," which introduced the cheerfully irritating creatures called the Preservers, as well as assorted supporting characters such as Malak, Selah and Olbar the Mountain-Tall (here, "Mountainous") in a story that works by itself, and also fits about midway through Volume Two of this series.

Front cover — Elfquest: Siege at Blue Mountain #5 (Warp Graphics)

Front cover — Elfquest: Siege at Blue Mountain #6 (Warp Graphics)

Front cover — Elfquest: Siege at Blue Mountain #7 (Warp Graphics)

Front cover — Elfquest: Siege at Blue Mountain #8 (Warp Graphics)

ONCE, THESE TINY, SEXLESS BEINGS CALLED THEMSELVES THE *PRESERVERS*...

BUT THAT WAS VERY LONG AGO, WHEN THEY COULD STILL REMEMBER WHO AND **WHY** THEY WERE!

NOW THEY SPIN THEIR SHIMMERING WEBS WITHOUT RHYME OR REASON --

--AND THE VERDANT VALLEY IN WHICH THEY DWELL IS SILVERED OVER WITH MYRIAD LUSTROUS *COCOONS!*

COCOONS WHICH THE PRESERVERS TEND WITH INFINITE CARE --

--BUT WHICH NEVER, NEVER *HATCH!*

SKRASH!

WHUZZAT?!

THUD THUD

(GASP!)

BIGTHINGS!

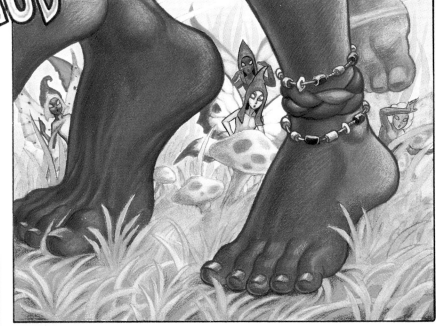

=PANT, PANT=
KEEP
RUNNING,
SELAH!

THIS
IS THE
FORBIDDEN
GROVE!

THEY WILL NOT
FOLLOW US HERE!

LOOK! BIGTHINGS
MESSING UP OUR
HANGEY-DOWNS!

AGH! THE
TREES THEM-
SELVES TRY TO
SNARE US!

I-I CANNOT
BEAR THE
TOUCH OF
THESE STICKY
WEBS!

MALAK,
HELP
ME!

FORGIVE ME!
NEVER BEFORE
HAVE I SQUIRMED
LIKE A CHILD AT
THE WORK OF
A SPIDER!

YOU ARE
BRAVER THAN
I, SELAH!

SEE
HOW I
TREMBLE!

ARE YOU NOT **SORRY** THAT YOU RAN AWAY WITH AN **OUTCAST?**

I **FAILED** MY TRIAL OF MANHOOD!

WHY ARE YOU NOT ASHAMED OF ME?

BECAUSE I **LOVE** YOU, GENTLE ONE!

AND NO MATTER **WHAT** OUR TRIBAL LAWS SAY --

--I WILL MAKE YOU A MAN --**NOW!**

LULLED INTO A MOMENT'S BLISS BY THE STILLNESS AND GOSSAMER BEAUTY OF THE PLACE --

--MALAK AND SELAH ARE OBLIVIOUS TO ALL BUT THEIR OWN ENFLAMED SENSES!

SHADE AND SWEET WATER!